Dr Sherwood is a psychotherapist and counsellor, and has published widely in these fields with a focus on the artistic therapies. She is passionate about human biography and the struggle to create meaning out of chaos, peace out of war and triumph over adversity. She is a second-generation migrant from Europe living in Australia in the countryside, with a great love for the natural environment.

To my maternal grandfather, Alfio; and my maternal grandmother, Maria, whose courage, integrity, wisdom, pioneering spirit and love of beauty, peace and freedom I have inherited.

Patricia Sherwood

ENEMY ALIEN NO. 72

AUSTIN MACAULEY PUBLISHERS™

LONDON · CAMBRIDGE · NEW YORK · SHARJAH

A CIP catalogue record for this title is available from the British Library.

ISBN 9781528906944 (Paperback)
ISBN 9781528906951 (E-Book)

www.austinmacauley.com

First Published (2019)
Austin Macauley Publishers Ltd
25 Canada Square
Canary Wharf
London
E14 5LQ

My deepest thanks to Jean Butler, the senior historian at the State Library of Western Australia, who inspired me to write this book, having viewed and archived a wide collection of my mother's papers and writings about her life. Gratitude is due to Janet Ristic for her dedicated assistance with editing and her reflective insights and conversations during the writing process.

Preface

Lina, my mother, migrated to Australia from Sicily in 1929. From a country whose soil was bloodied by generations of violence, poverty and political oppression, her family sought peace, freedom and prosperity as far as possible away from Fascist Italy. Lina's dream was to become a teacher. Despite the tragedies of her childhood including the witnessed murder of her mother, her poverty, rural isolation, barriers of ethnicity and language, her will and resilience were inspirational. At 18 years of age, in 1939, she was declared, 'enemy alien no. 72' because Australia was at war with Fascist Italy.

Despite restrictions upon her movement, daily police surveillance, and prejudice, she became the first Italian woman migrant in Western Australia to become a school teacher. She taught for thirty eight years: 12 years as a teacher in rural schools and 26 years in metropolitan primary schools in Western Australia.

Many of her other dreams of living in a harmonious and peaceful family and community were severely challenged throughout her life. Her marriage to a WW2 veteran was troubled throughout its 35 years as they both wrestled in their own ways with the stresses of the wars that they had survived. Her commitment to motherhood led to years of abuse, intentional or otherwise, by her son who turned from genius into madman in the course of his adulthood. Yet despite these adversities weighing like chains around her ankles, her enduring spirit was never defeated. She was the guardian of a largely refugee migrant neighbourhood, providing support, advice, literacy and compassion for these 'new Australians' as they transited into Australian culture, a transition that she had made alone so many years before in her family's search for freedom and peace from political oppression.

Lina also shone her light into the hearts and minds of hundreds of school children during her 38 year teaching career in rural and urban Western Australia where she created classrooms of beauty, goodness, learning and tranquillity that students remembered fondly as adults. Her love of Australia, the country that become her home and to whom she gave her heart, was reflected in the many splendid landscapes that she painted; of golden deserts, rugged mountains, vast wheat fields, and azure sparkling waters of this land. She remains an inspiration to all of us who dare to dream to become the best of who we are even in adverse conditions.

Without doubt, she was gifted, intelligent, artistic, creative and resilient. What is most outstanding, though, is her stoicism, her tremendous courage and determination in the face of even the most acute challenges to not surrender; to not admit defeat, hopelessness or despair. Lina's strength derived from her marriage to goodness, to honesty, kindness and her willingness to forbear injustice with patience and tolerance and to choose to find a place of understanding and forgiveness for those whose deeds had caused her harm. Always she sought a pathway to peace even amid the violence that erupted in her life. Her strength was inherited from her remarkable father, a man of integrity and goodness and to generations of her Sicilian ancestors who despite aeons of violence and political oppression created a culture with profound elements of beauty, goodness, resilience and hope.

Table of Contents

Chapter 1
Rekindling Hope

Alfio held his new-born daughter Lina close to his heart as Maria, his beloved wife, rested after the labour. He had delivered a beautiful girl, whom they named Lucia, 'the light', but whom they called Lina. This little one, although his third daughter, was special, a symbol of new hope as a family for peace together. Having survived conscription into the Italian army, in a futile war in northern Italy during 1915–1918, he had returned to his beloved wife and two daughters as a man who cherished every moment alive, every day he could spend with his family. He had seen so much death and suffering, he valued each moment of life and now this new baby, Lina, represented their post war dreams of peace and uninterrupted contentment.

It was 1921, a hot August day as he gazed out of their beautiful home nestled on the slopes of Mount Etna in the little village of Monterosso. He mused upon the towering, threatening beauty of Mount Etna, unpredictably on the verge of explosiveness with its violent lava flows but providing fertile soil for cultivation of grapes, citrus, fruits, vegetables, chestnuts, almonds and pistachios upon which they depended for a good life. Lina would continue generations of his family who had lived here on these volcanic slopes with vistas to the sparkling Ionian Sea abounding with fish. He prayed in his heart that she would live in country free of war and violence that had plagued his beautiful homeland, Sicily for interminable generations upon generations.

He considered himself a fortunate man, fortunate to be alive and fortunate to have married Maria. He was a humble cattle dealer, with two years of schooling only; as his family were not wealthy and schooling where it existed cost money. In his youth bandits, the dreaded 'bandista', who were comprised primarily of the desperate rural poor who robbed and marauded villages mostly for food to ward of starvation, had ambushed him while he was moving his cattle to another grazing field. They had tied him up and placed a loaded gun under his neck so that if he moved he would die. He had prayed then and his prayers were heard, as a passer-by was alerted by his shouts and released him.

He had prayed, too, for a good wife and the answer came unexpectedly. He had seen Maria with her father outside the family vineyards on a visit to Monterosso and he knew immediately that he loved her. This love was deep and fathomless. It had taken his whole body, mind and soul by surprise. He had not known this love before. It was as if he had known her for aeons. In the usual circumstances, he would not be eligible to even consider her, as her family were very wealthy middle class, owning orchards, vineyards, chestnut groves and shops. Descendants from the French invasions of Sicily, they had land, wealth and status. He knew she has been to a school for gifted mathematicians; she had a younger sister, Lucia, married to the head of the Sicilian 'Cabinari' or police force. She had two brothers, one who owned a shop, Giuliano; another, Marcu, who had travelled to America. However, she had been kidnapped at 12 years of age and although she had not been raped, she had not been chaperoned, so was no longer eligible to marry in her class. Her distraught father had gone searching for his beloved daughter and found her wandering the coastline near Stazzo where she had landed after jumping out of her kidnapper's boat and making it to shore. Rumours had it that her mother had organised the kidnapping to relieve the family of paying substantial dowry for Maria, her eldest daughter whom she disliked intensely. Alfio asked for her hand in marriage and it was given to him. To Maria's mother's chagrin, they were immeasurably happy. Alfio reminisced how he and his wife of almost 20 years had never argued, and that they had a marriage of equals together making the decisions for their family. Well not quite equals, because he knew she was his sun, and his life revolved around her. She was the centre of his world, the purpose and meaning of his life and when hungry, cold and afraid in those cold nights during the War, it was focusing upon her warmth, her love, her body, that kept him alive and determined to return home. She was the mother of his three beautiful daughters and they had dreams together to raise their girls in peace and prosperity, in integrity and freedom.

He could never understand the wars that families ran. There were enough wars on a national scale, he thought, but here he was caught up in a family war against his beloved Maria. Her father had been a good man, nicknamed 'the monk'. Wealthy and married to a dominating and manipulating woman, he chose to spend most of his time in the church. He loved his daughter Maria dearly but could not stand up to his wife's dislike of Maria, so in his will had left a particular property to her to compensate for the dowry she had not received. He died young, not yet sixty, in a region where no one was called old until they reached 100 years. Maria's mother, Elena, lived next door to them, so often they went to visit. She taunted Alfio, claiming that she was 'bringing up his children' which struck a blow to his pride. It was not true, he worked hard for his family, and his wife Maria had a shop where she sold small goods, wine and tobacco and he worked the chestnut groves, the vineyards and the properties to provide for his family. Finally, after prolonged 'insults' from her mother who seemed jealous of her happy marriage, Maria had told her mother that she must cease such unfair conversation and the silent family war which was to have bitter casualties began as her mother refused thereafter to speak to them. Alfio had seen life at its most precarious during the war and was bewildered that Maria's family, with so much wealth and comfort, could be so warlike and so driven by greed and enmity. His mother was poor, but she loved all her children warmly and his family had shared generously whatever material goods they possessed.

15

He remembered, in the fibre of his soul, these qualities and vowed to give them to his family.

Lina was soon walking and exploring her world with gusto. She loved the beautiful chestnut forest backing onto their home, and would wander through it collecting bunches of beautiful pink cyclamens while her family collected chestnuts and wood. She lived in her family's warmth, with freedom and love that nurtured her pioneering spirit. One day though, seeking a castle that she was certain was in the chestnut grove, she became thoroughly lost. Her father found her just as the cold dark evening began setting in. She knew he would always come and find her. It was like the day when her mother was so busy in the shop, serving customers, that she wandered into the cellar beneath the shop where all the wine for sale was stored. Lina thought she would drink some wine like her parents did with the evening meal, so she opened a bottle and began to drink the sweet red liquid. Soon, she was in a drunken stupor and, with her wobbly legs, could not walk the 100 steps upwards and out of the cellar. She could not understand why she kept rolling backwards and eventually collapsed on the ground exhausted and settled in for a deep sleep. The family were alerted that Lina had disappeared again. The forest, her favourite haunt was searched to no avail. No one could find her. Just before the evening meal when her father came down to collect the wine he discovered her, and his heart burst with gratitude as he lifted the little one who was 'lost' into his arms and carried her up the steps of the cellar which her intoxicated legs could no longer climb. Never did he scold her, or any of his children, so great was his value for life that no matter what mishap, what disaster occurred large or small, he would always comment, "But we are alive and we have each other. Nothing else is important."

Lina was four years old when she returned with her sisters from mass on St Peter's day to welcome her new baby sister, Rosanna. She loved her dearly but was not so pleased that she now had to share the special place in her mother and father's bed with her baby sister especially when she was peed upon. Her mother would tell her to go to her older sister's room at night, but she often missed her parents and would come creeping into her father's side of the bed. He would make a cradle with his arms outside of the bed until Lina fell asleep then place her gently in bed. She knew she had a special place in his heart.

Alfio did not greet Rosanna's birth in 1925 with the same hope and joyful optimism for peace, he had held when Lina was born. Storm clouds were gathering on the home front and the political horizon. At home, his mother-in-law had not spoken to them for four years despite his wife's attempts to restore peace. The girls had been told that they were to visit her only with one of their parents and it was difficult for Lina. He sometimes saw his mother-in-law poking biscuits through slits in the fence and calling, "Lina, Lina come over here and play." He could not understand such on-going hostility to her own daughter but apparent interest in enticing Lina to disobey her mother. However, the threat of war on the community and political level was of far greater concern to him. As a man committed to freedom and peace, he ardently disliked Mussolini. "That man is a madman. He will lead us to another war and I will not fight another war," he would say to the family. Sicilians, like Alfio, particularly resented Italian rule with its accompanying conscription of their men. They had lived through thousands of years of invaders and the Italians were the only ones that enforced conscription upon them causing great hardship to their largely agrarian economy and labour force. The appointment of Mori by Mussolini in 1925, to eradicate the mafia in Sicily using unlimited force was implemented ruthlessly and indiscriminately throughout Sicily. There were random raids on villages, trumped up arrests, fake trials and incredible suffering for the Sicilian communities. Alfio, with peace, justice and individual freedom as the fibres of his being, was very distressed by these repressive, controlling, unjust behaviours of the fascist polity. The joy of community life where families spent long summer evenings strolling in the piazzas and sharing communal meals, conversations and activities was profoundly impacted. A man could be randomly arrested in a street for speaking to another man. Mori, either did not know or did not care to identify the mafia accurately and any Sicilian man's life was at stake. For Sicilians this was like a second 'Inquisition'. Alfio shuddered as he thought how much freedom had been lost in the four years since Mussolini had come to power, and he feared greatly for the future now that Mussolini had declared himself dictator of Italy and elections had been abolished.

The final straw was the militarisation of his children. School uniform was now black skirts, white blouses and black kerchiefs. It disturbed him to the core of his being to hear his beautiful Lina come home from school, gaily singing:

Liamo piccolo ballilla
Della patria figlioletti
Liamo la fossa dilspa
Domaniche Vittoria portera

(Translation)
We are small ballilla (fascists)
Children of our fatherland
We are tomorrow's strength
Who will be victorious.

He and Maria spent many quiet evenings after the children were asleep discussing their options. Like tens of thousands of other Sicilians who had borne the brunt of appalling neglect and exploitation by the government in Rome for decades, they decided that emigration was their best option. They would join his cousin in Western Australia who had emigrated in 1916 and who had become famous and prosperous as the 'Tomato King'. Here they would be out of the reaches of Mussolini and the fascist regime, and they could live a family life of peace, prosperity and freedom. They could educate their daughters and not worry about the size of dowries. Finally, Maria's mother had not spoken to her for years now and continued to ignore her if she tried to visit her. She had moved away to a neighbouring town and had given her son

Marcu, the neighbouring property. All things considered Alfio and Maria decided to immigrate to Australia in 1926.

They could live in peace without family or national discord. Alfio would go first, as was the Italian emigration pattern and obtain property and a house for the family. He would have to work hard for a year or so but when housing was ready, Maria would come with the children. In the meantime, she would sell up her personal properties and bring the monies to start their new life in Australia. It would be heartbreaking to leave this land of rare beauty, the chestnut groves, the familiarity of Mount Etna and the sparkling blue ocean, the rich volcanic soil upon which generations of his Greek Sicilian ancestors had lived but the time had come. He consoled himself that sometimes one's heart must break open to encompass new growth and this was in his best interests and the best interests of his family.

Lina was oblivious to these momentous decisions which would change her family and her life irreversibly. She glowed in the early years of childhood bathed in her mother and father's love. Her memories are of the beauty of the pink painted home facing the great Mount Etna. Her home was full of the smells of pizza, spaghetti and anchovies. It had brick-red floor tiles and beautiful furniture. She was entranced by the paintings of angels on the bed heads, the painting of a woman brushing her hair behind her mother's dressing table, the exquisite delicate china and her mother's jewellery. Her mother bathed her in beauty and she treasured her pretty dresses, her little pink umbrella with bicycles on it, which she used when she walked the six kilometres to the coast with her mother to buy fish.

Her mother was warm and loving and never scolded her even when she stole her tomahawk from the shop and cut her finger badly while trying to chop wood. The community of children playing in the streets while the mothers chatted in the evening was cherished by Maria and delighted in by Lina as she found childhood friends with whom to play games. Lina also loved the village church with its remarkable mosaics and paintings, and she would sit for hours with her mother and other women from the village while they crocheted angels and duplicated frescoes in their crocheted table cloths. She imagined that one day she would be a painter and paint frescos for the women to crochet as patterns. Everywhere her world was rich with love and warmth, community and friendship. In her childhood innocence, she did not notice discord except in the occasional arguments with her older sister Elena who had the task of caring for her when her mother was very busy. Like Elena, she was strong and independently minded, and the two often clashed. Lina simply would not do what Elena commanded her to do sometimes and Elena would give her the odd smack, which she would report to her parents. They would both be told quietly, "Arguing and smacking is not permitted in their family." It is a home of peace not violence.

Lina's world changed when she was five years old. She was told that her father would be leaving for a faraway land and they would be leaving Sicily to join him in a year or two. Her paternal grandmother came to say goodbye to him and cried as she clung to him weeping, "I will never see you again," which was the great grief of the parents of emigrants in Sicily. Lina's mother cried for hours after she had said goodbye to Alfio, not knowing that she would never see him again either. Lina was distressed and confused. She has never seen her mother upset and crying and her little heart sank. What did it all mean? She was soon to learn as her older sisters Elena and Marina busied themselves helping their mother with the many chores their father had once done.

Soon there was packing up, and selling off surplus household items. Passports were being prepared. She, Elena and Rosanna would travel on their mother's passport and their oldest sister Marina who was 19 years of age would have her own passport. They would be ready to join their father when he had prepared a house for them. Lina understood it would be a long journey of eight to twelve weeks to the other side of the world, far, far away from everything she knew in Sicily. Her parents had told her that she would be going to a new land, a land of peace, prosperity and freedom. She hoped they were right.

Chapter 2
Shattering the Dream

Lina was picking cyclamens again in the chestnut forest on the slopes of Mount Etna where it is said that Hades kidnapped Persephone as she gathered flowers and incarcerated her in the hell realms. Lina's mother called her home. She had important paperwork to finalise as her property sales were now almost completed and she would take Lina with her to the government offices in Catania. Lina could sense her mother's excitement at the prospect of setting sail soon to join her father but she also could feel her mother's weariness. Her mother always seemed busy these days working in her shop, doing paperwork or looking after Rosanna who was now three years old. While preparing to go to Catania with her mother, Uncle Marcu arrived. Lina's heart sank. She did not understand the conversation but she could sense his anger and rage directed towards her mother and she could hear him repeat, "Give me the title deeds to the property our father gave you. You will never sell it. It belongs to our family."

Maria refused politely but firmly. "This property," she replied, "is mine, I have the title deeds in my name and it was given to me by my father. I am leaving the country and I am now selling it. You do not have any legal rights to this property."

Marcu then yelled, "Well, if you don't give it to me I am going home to get a gun, and I will shoot you and take the title deeds." Lina did not know what a gun was exactly but she felt frightened by his rage and anger. Lina's mother remained calm and comforted Lina saying, "He does not really mean it. We are brother and sister. We have no fight between us."

Maria had lost touch with Marcu. He was her oldest brother and although they had shared childhoods, his adult life was a mystery to her. She knew as a young man he had been desperately in love with a local woman but their mother had refused to allow the marriage because the girl's family had insufficient dowry. He had disappeared for some years to New York at their mother's expense. No one knew what he did there though it was rumoured that he had become involved with the mafia. He had returned to Sicily, been given the property next to Maria by their mother and lived a reclusive life, still without a wife, without obvious work but with visits to New York. What Maria underestimated was the strength of her mother's influence over Marcu. Their mother had for years been poisoning his mind with her hatred and jealousy of Maria. There was a potent alliance between them against Maria and their agreement was that Maria was to be stripped of the title deeds to her property at all costs. The property was not to leave the family and Maria was not to leave Sicily and join her husband in Australia at any cost even if the cost was her death.

Lina was holding her mother's left hand, little baby Rosanna was held in her right arm as she walked down the street. Marcu came up behind her and began firing his shotgun repetitively into her back. He shot her twelve times at point blank range. Elena, now 15 years of age, tried to stop him in his shooting frenzy but he pushed her to the ground. Maria laid writhing and screaming on the ground crying, "My life is over, take care of your selves." It was August 15th, 1928 and the church bells rang out in the village for the feast of Assumption into heaven of the Blessed Virgin Mary. However, the saints did not hear on that day and Maria was not relieved in her agony of a quick death. In a community without hospitals and doctors, it took ten days for her to die in the family home alternating between screaming in pain, prolonged moaning and becoming motionless. Lina was terrified. She so wanted to touch her mother and hug her but the blood, the screaming, the ghostly white of her face were so unfamiliar to her that she froze. All that Lina could focus upon in those long days and nights of her mother's dying were the church bells, like clockwork, every 15 minutes were rung out by the bells day and night, night and day. It was ten days and nights of tracking the ringing bells before Maria mercifully died. Lina did not speak or eat for many days so great was this explosive shock to her little body. Now she had no mother, and a father so far away, people called her an orphan. She had seen orphans in the street. They were hungry, dirty and sad. Rosanna kept crying for her mother. She did not understand that she was dead. Lina tried to hold her hand and comfort her. Elena seemed desperately pre-occupied. Marina who was 19 years old remained very quiet. She had been ill for many years with scarlet fever and her health was fragile. She tried to comfort Rosanna as well. The funeral in the village church was a depressing affair. The whole village turned out shocked by the murder of a 'good wife and mother' by her brother. Murders in Sicily were not uncommon but the murder of a sister by a brother was an unspeakable 'family shame' because the family was sacrosanct. Outsiders might be murdered, but family members should always be honoured. There were no words for it. Lina remembered having all her beautiful dresses that her mother had made for her taken away and being made to wear black, black every day, everywhere for two whole years as was the custom in Sicily when a parent died. Lina's joyful rainbow world of childhood finished abruptly as her mother's funeral was on her seventh birthday.

Elena, still only 15 years of age, had to make important decisions about their welfare. The murder had been publically witnessed in the village just outside their home and it was to go to court for he had been charged with wilful murder. Elena's life was now also under threat as she would be the key witness, having heard the original threat to kill her mother and having witnessed the follow up murder. A black car had come to their village with men looking for Elena who fortunately had been away visiting relatives in another village. She knew they must leave their beautiful home and go into hiding. The only relative willing and able to assist was their father's brother Uncle Guiseppe and his wife Aunt Magdelena who lived in Pisano, a village further down the slopes of Mount Etna. Elena knew it was not the best decision as he was a notorious gambler but it was their only option. She could stay in hiding at Aunt Magdelena's appearing in public only for the court hearing. In addition, Aunt Magdelena's two sons had left home one to become a priest in Rome, the other studying the law, so there was space in the house for the four girls.

Lina's joyful childhood changed overnight as Aunt Magdelena was neither loving, kind nor joyful like her mother. She was bitter woman burnt out by managing a household whose finances were always precarious because of her husband's gambling addiction. She said that there was no time for childhood play and Lina was set to work, learning to knit stockings, sew clothes and crochet bedspreads. Lina had never done any such tasks in childhood and was admonished by her Aunt for her lack of skill. Aunt Magdelena boasted that she had crocheted a whole bedspread when she was four years old. Lina's heart, frozen in shock and grief for the loss of her mother crumpled into despair but her hands and legs were kept busy by Aunt Magdelena's demands. Not only did she have to knit and sew and crochet but also she had to run all errands outside of the house as Elena was in hiding and Marina could not leave the house. At lunchtime, she had to carry the lunches to the men working in the fields despite her terror of the dogs that lived upon the way. If she stopped to pick bunches of violets on her way home, flowers being her only joy, she would be chastised for taking too long. There were shopping errands to run, floors to sweep and yards to clean. Lina's life had become one long list of cold, disheartening chores without relief. She wondered if her father would ever come, find her, and take her in his arms home, as he used to when she was lost as a child. She could not even name her fear of being left in this place with the cold, authoritarian Aunt Magdelena. In addition, she worried for Rosanna, always a fussy eater. Her mother would accommodate her but Aunt Magdelena would not give her any food at all until she finished what was on her plate. Rosanna particularly refused to eat salty anchovies and would cry for hours and hours with hunger. She would beg Lina for bread and Lina would try to save her bread from her meal to feed her sister. She feared Rosanna might die from lack of food. Every day when they said the rosary as a household, she would pray reverently to Mary that her father would come and take them all away with him, very soon before any more of them died. The church bells rang out across the village every 15 minutes. Lina decided that she would remind Mary and Jesus every 15 minutes that she needed her father.

Attempts to kidnap Elena prior to the court hearing failed. Accused of wilful murder Marcu pleaded in his defence that it was an honour killing because Maria was a 'bad, immoral woman who was bringing shame upon the family name' and therefore he should be acquitted. However, they were unable to produce any evidence at all to support the case. Elena described his first visit and demand for the title deeds and the second visit in which he followed out his threat to kill his sister. Marcu was convicted of wilful murder and given a prison sentence of twenty years. There were no winners in this case as the four girls had lost their mother, regardless of the court outcome, but at least justice was seen to be done, which was not always the case in Sicily. The outcome was a ragged victory for justice.

Alfio had worked very hard for over a year and had purchased ten acres of orchard with a shanty type of house in Newlands, Western Australia. He was had spent many days labouring in the hot sun motivated by the dream of being re-united at last with his beloved Maria and his four beautiful daughters. Of late, he had been feeling disquiet but he had assumed that it was because he was uncertain as to how the family would adjust to the poverty of their life in Australia with the very poor house he had managed to buy. Then one day a letter arrived unexpectedly from Elena. It was his wife Maria that usually wrote the letters to him. The letter was dated August 1928. It was now November 1928. He read Elena's news of Maria's death with disbelief and then his heart broke with the weight of his grief and shock, and then the self-recriminations. If only he had been there, he could have fought off her brother, perhaps it would not have happened. He would have given his life to defend Maria; no cost to him to save her would have been too great. But now she was dead and at the hand of her own brother with her mother's complicity. How does a man make sense of such hatred and greed? He had seen greed before in his life and watched it destroy the humanity of people. He remembered the great 1908 Messina earthquake in Sicily when tens of thousands of people lost their lives and the living ones driven by greed, crawling over dead bodies cutting off gold earrings and necklaces. He felt ill just remembering the lack of humanity, the lack of respect for these human beings who had died so tragically. He knew how greed de-humanised people, but hatred – family hatred – how does a man make sense of this? If it were only greed, Marcu could have walked into their house, overpowered his wife physically, she was just over five feet tall and he was a big man. He could easily have taken the title deeds. It was an easy task. A woman with two small children clinging to her was an easy target. But her murder, this was hatred, pure hatred, as dark as hatred can be…he did not know the nature of such a beast, nor did he have a revengeful bone in his body. He only knew that those treating others with such hatred must live with their own hatred, which must poison their souls with darkness and metamorphose into self-hatred. Nor did it give him any joy when five years later he was to learn that Marcu had hung himself in prison and his mother-in-law had gone quite mad shortly after hearing that news and was incarcerated in a home for the mentally unstable.

Maria, his sun, the centre of his universe was gone. The aching well of darkness in his soul knew no relief. She who was his most precious friend, wife and companion was no longer. He had never cried as a man, but now he cried, wrenching anguished tears that would never be dried. He was gutted. Her warmth, love and touch had filled his life with purpose and passion but now it was all demolished. Only their children were left amid the ruins. He must live for them now.

The letters continued to arrive. One from his brother Giuseppe explaining that they had taken over the care of his children and the protection of Elena for the court hearing and for consent to use the family monies for the court hearing and the costs of housing and feeding his four daughters. They offered to adopt Rosanna as Aunt Magdelena had always fancied having a daughter and could no longer have children. They asked him what he would like them to do with the remaining three girls. Alfio was mortified, horrified and appalled at their insensitivity about his daughters. To suggest that they keep Rosanna and dispose of his daughters, like cattle was unthinkable. He had delivered each one of these beautiful girls and they were his co-creations with his beloved Maria. They were all he had left of her presence in his life. He wrote back a very stern letter agreeing to their financial control of the monies even knowing that his brother was a chronic gambler. The heart of the letter though was his command that all of his daughters join him in Australia as soon as possible following the court hearing. To underline the importance of ALL of his daughters, he added 'and send my cat as well'. He felt at times that the grief of his loss was so great that he could die easily of a broken heart but his will was not broken and his love for his four daughters kept him alive and working. He must now build a better world for them. He would pick up the pieces of his shattered dream with Maria to build a better future for their daughters and he would endure any hardship to make their lives better. He would not give up. That is what Maria would have liked. She was never fearful, or defeatist. She always stood courageously by his side and encouraged him. He would not give up now. They could murder her body, take her beauty and her physical presence from him, but they could never take her spirit and the memories of her warmth, beauty and goodness. He held her in his hearten sacred ground, where no other person would ever come.

After the court hearing and the response from their father the girls were advised they would be joining him in Australia, Lina was overjoyed. The blessed Mary had heard her prayers. Lina could stop counting the church bells. However, Uncle

Giuseppe had squandered the estate and now had no money left for their fares to Australia. He procrastinated saying they needed new passports, which was true. Lina and her sister Rosanna as minors would now enter Australia as the children of their oldest sister Marina who had just turned 20 years of age. Elena who was now 16 years of age would now enter Australia on her own passport.

Meanwhile the months passed and Lina and Elena continued to attend school, both of them proving to be outstanding students. Lina's reports were praiseworthy to say the least and she made her first holy communion in the little church at Pisano. When her mother was alive, Lina rarely concentrated at school. She would say to her teacher, "I don't like *A's* and I won't write *a's*," and would play around in class. Now life was deadly serious. It was survival and learning to read and write well was part of it. Her older sister, Elena, who was very gifted reminded Lina daily of the need to do well at school and make her father proud. Finally, Uncle Giuseppe had run out of excuses as to why the girls could not immigrate to Australia, so he set off with the four of them saying he would be able to borrow money for their fares from a priest friend in Naples. They had to travel by road to Messina and then by boat across the tumultuous Ionian Sea, where the feared Cyclopean monsters lived and fought under the waves, all the way to Calabria Reggio. Then a train journey to the port of Naples. In Naples, they were to board the Marconi and begin their eight-week voyage to Australia. On arriving in Naples, Uncle Giuseppe's friend was unable or unwilling to loan him the money for their passages to Australia so Uncle Giuseppe dropped the four girls off at the Naples seaport without tickets and wished them well. Elena, now 16 decided that she must find a way to get them to Australia. She waited unit she saw some of her cousins depositing change in their wallets after paying for their passages and she begged them to loan it to them, promising that her father would pay it back to them after they arrived in Australia. Fortunately, her father had a reputation as an honest man of his word, the money was loaned, and the tickets purchased.

Lina, now eight years old, remembered vividly the long passage to Australia. She and her sisters dressed in black, sitting on the deck all crying for their lost mother. Her little four-year-old sister Rosanna was treated kindly by an English couple who gave her sweets and played games with her. Lina was entranced by the endless yellow sand as they passaged through the Suez Canal, and the brightly coloured necklaces and wares of the Arabs when they docked into port, captured her imagination. She knew that one day she would paint deserts of golden sands like this. Then so much blue water, she liked the blue water. It reminded her of the ocean at Stazzo where she and her mother would go to buy fish. Then this new country called India with so many brightly clad people with saris of all beautiful colours as the ship docked at Bombay. Lina wished she could wear one of those brightly coloured saris. She hated the ugly black dress that she was made to wear every day. Lina was sure that her mother would not have wanted her to wear black. She would have wanted her to wear beautiful clothes full of the colours she could see around her. Every day she went to English lessons with her sisters and she tried very hard to learn this new language. Then one day, the strange smell of eucalyptus, not like lemon or bergamot with which she was familiar, floated across the waves. The passengers were told, "This is the smell of Australia, you are very close now." By the time the ship came to harbour in Fremantle, Western Australia, she could not speak English but she could understand it a little. As she looked down on Fremantle wharf, she was sure she could see her father. She knew he would come, find her, and take her home. He had never failed but his time it seemed like it had taken him such a long time to find her. When she saw him though, she did not run to greet him, as she would have done a few years before, but she walked deliberately and tentatively towards him following her bigger sisters, the four of them like a black chain slowly uncoiling towards him in the distance.

Alfio was overjoyed to see them and despite the bad news about them bringing no money from the family property with them, and he being in debt for their passages to Australia he was overjoyed "You are alive," he said, "I am alive, we are together, nothing else matters." Core to his values was the preciousness of human life. It had always been that way but now it was even stronger. Therefore, the three-hour trip home was shared stories of the tragedy of the last year without their mother and of their relief to be a family again. Lina sat closest to her father. She was frightened by the strange trees and bird sounds around them. The endless forests seemed to overwhelm her and the orange red gravel road was a beautiful colour but very bumpy. When they finally arrived, it was to a little shed with fruit boxes for seats, one big bed for all the girls to share while their father slept on a canvas camper's bed. There was one little wood stove in the kitchen, one little wooden table, one old sewing machine and outside the strangest sound during the nights, like thumping on the ground. Lina was glad she was sleeping next to Elena. She would keep her safe in this strange land. Lina wondered why her parents had given up all the beauty in their homeland for this ugly little house and this strange countryside. When spring arrived and the wildflowers bloomed, Lina was happy and she began to draw them with delight. Flowers always made her happy. Especially she loved the golden wattle, each flower like a little sun, golden, round, and bursting with light. There were strange red and green kangaroo paws, spider orchards, enamel orchards and all sorts of rare and wonderful flowers, which entranced her sense of beauty and her childhood creativity. She would draw them, take them into her heart, and place them inside her home. She would make this country her home. The gum leaves became her paper. She would dry them and flatten them and then she would paint and draw these beautiful coloured birds and flowers she saw around her upon them. She would search for large round smooth rocks in the creek and these too were her artist's paper. She painted little possums, rabbits and goannas on these rocks. Nature was her solace and her healer and she was fast making friends with this new country.

Chapter 3
Keeping the Peace

The jarrah forests did not seem friendly like the chestnut groves at home, and they did not provide food to eat. Lina noticed how hard her father worked with an axe and when he could afford it gelignite to clear the forest to make way for a potato crop or tomato crop or fruit trees. He was in debt for their passage so was working hard to harvest a good potato crop so he could pay off his debts. Elena and Marina, now adults, had to help work in the orchards and clearing the land. They were busy from dawn to dusk with a siesta just after their midday meal, in keeping with their tradition of work at home. Lina and her sister, Rosanna were free to be children again and to play. Lina especially loved the little creek that ran through the back of their orchard where a big silver wattle tree grew and she spent many hours there with Rosanna becoming a wattle fairy and making a dress out of the golden wattle blossoms. Lina was soon enrolled to attend the local Newlands primary school. She remembers her first day vividly when she was told that her name was now 'Lucy' not 'Lina'. In her heart she knew that part of 'Lina' had already died with her mother in Sicily. Lucy was who she was going to be in this new country but now she still was really Lina.

The other children pointed at her and laughed saying in English, "Look at that little black thing." She could not speak English but she understood a great deal. Lina was shamed when she completed her mathematics sheet and the teacher asked the girl sitting next to her if she had cheated and the girl replied, "No, Lucy cheated." She was deeply shamed. She had never cheated but she did not have words to speak up for herself in English. She would never cheat because her father and her mother would be very ashamed of her. They always said that honesty and integrity is very important. It means you can look another human being in the eye and sleep peacefully at night. Lina did not know how she could sleep peacefully with all these children pointing at her. She did not want to be different but she could not talk to them yet and she did not know their games. She was happy when her father said Rosanna could come to school with her too. Rosanna was only four years old but there was no one to look after her during the day so she was best at school. It was a one-teacher school with 15 children from four years of age to 12 years of age. All the boys liked Rosanna because she was very pretty and very cute and they piggy backed her around the school yard because she was so little. Soon, Lina learned English, rapidly in fact, because she knew she needed to help her father as well when he went shopping. He would say, "Lina, you are so clever, you learn so fast." She learned English so fast that soon the teacher realised she was a gifted child. Within one year of arrival in Australia, aged nine years, she won the state prize for the best hand drawn map of Western Australia by a primary school student. Not only was it drawn as if photographed, but every river and major town was beautifully written in perfect English in black ink. By the end of her first year at school, she won the prize for the most gifted academic student. Her artwork was of exhibition standard. Never had the teachers seen a child with such artistic abilities. Lina still wore black to school but now the children stopped pointing at her and she had many friends. Lina had come to understand this country with its stark bright blue skies and dark green jarrah forests; it was reflected in her artwork together with an array of native animals such as kangaroos, kookaburras and emus.

Alfio was proud of Lina and he could rely on her to translate when they went shopping for essential farm items. The Great depression had hit, potatoes were being dumped in the ocean off the jetty in Bunbury because markets had collapsed. Consequently, they were very, very poor. They subsisted on home grown vegetables, fruits, green weeds, kangaroos, 28 parrots, chickens and eggs and considered themselves fortunate. Lining the roadside were the mass of unemployed sustenance workers with their families living in tents that would come to their door begging for apples that had fallen on the ground. These were hard times, very hard times. Alfio sold his best suit to obtain money to start to pay for the girl's passages to Australia because the potato markets had collapsed.

Alfio was an enigma even to his Sicilian neighbouring orchardists. They recognised him to be a man of integrity and honesty but they wondered why he was liberal with his adult daughters, always giving them the full rights to make decisions over their lives especially in relation to whom they married. Marina, who was 20 years old, married shortly after her arrival in Australia to another Sicilian orchardist in a neighbouring town. Elena, who was now 17 years of age, was running the household and caring for Lina and Rosanna. She had fallen deeply in love with a local orchardist who Alfio knew well. This was a dilemma for him because he deeply believed in the individuals' freedom to direct their own lives and his daughters freedom to choose to marry whom they so desired. He was not a traditionalist, nor a feminist. He was a humanist believing profoundly in individual freedom and the dignity of each person to freely choose their destiny. However, he had worked with this man and found him to be very ill tempered. He pointed this out to Elena, saying that although he was a hard worker, he could be very hot tempered. She insisted that she loved him regardless, so he replied, "I would not marry him if he was covered with gold dust, but it is your life and your choice. Whatever you decide you have my blessing." Elena decided to marry him, so Alfio was now faced with the difficult task of who would care for Lina and Rosanna who were now eight and four years old. Alfio then called Elena and her potential spouse together and said that they must wait two years until Lina was ten years old and sufficiently grown to run the household and care for Rosanna. During this time, he advised Elena's prospective partner to build a house for her and their future family to be.

Therefore, it came about that at ten years of age Lina's childhood finished abruptly and she became responsible for running the household. Cooking, shopping, washing the clothes, ironing the clothes, preparing Rosanna and herself for school. She was also responsible for taking care of Rosanna who had long since regarded her as her mother as well as her sister, as memories of her own mother had long vanished. Alfio's heart was torn between anguish and joy. His two oldest girls would have hard lives, they would work the land with their partners. They would never have had to work outside in the farms in Sicily. They were however in a free country, far away from war and fascism, and they were young and they had the opportunity to prosper and make good lives for themselves and their children. It was Lina's destiny that troubled him most. Lina had always been the child of promise, born at that time when he and Maria's lives were so full of hope and promise for themselves and their families. Lina was so like Maria in character and appearance. She had her intelligence, her artistry, her capacity to create beauty, her determination and her kindness. Yet she was so small, already burdened with so many household duties at ten years of age, that he wondered how her spirit would cope. She was fast becoming his right hand because working on the farm made it impossible for him to learn English. She was his interpreter, completed any paperwork for him and now she was running the household and caring for Rosanna. He was so proud of her, each year she would gain the best academic student award as well as the hygiene prize for the child with the neatest hair, cleanest nails and shoes in the school. Lina had courage, determination and will like her mother. He would encourage her as he encouraged all of his daughters to be the best person they could be. "Lina," he would affirm, "you are so clever, you will be a wonderful teacher," when she expressed her desire to become a school teacher. Yet in his heart he wondered about her future in this unknown land and this unknown culture.

Lina loved school and every piece of schoolwork whether written or drawing, needlecraft or oral work, Lina devoted herself to doing it perfectly. Lina had a deep moral core where doing you best was the only thing that was good enough. One did not do one's best for material reward, one did it because it was the fulfilment of your humanity and you owed it the other people in your world to be the best human being possible. Despite experiences of betrayal, hatred, and greed that had marred her early childhood, like her father, she did not allow this to tarnish the core of her integrity as a human being. Her heart would always grieve these injustices but they would never contaminate her moral core. She would be honest, kind, compassionate and live with integrity like her father. As he had often said to her, "People may destroy your outer possessions, even the people you most love but always maintain you integrity and goodness. They must never reduce to their level of greed, hatred or jealousy."

On the home front the challenges for Lina were daily. Carting the washing to the creek to scrub it on washing boards and dry it in the sun. Cooking meals from food largely gathered from the garden, cleaning the old house and worrying about Dad if he came home late from the orchards or the paddocks. Whenever she felt overwhelmed, she would run over to her sister Elena's house and ask for help. Elena had become her mother. Lina looked to her for advice and help with every household crisis. She wept with Elena when the cat stole the meat she had left on the kitchen table to cook for her father's dinner. Meat was a rarity so she was devastated that her neglect had caused such a problem. As was his stalwart character, Alfio never fussed over the minor things in life…he replied comfortingly, "You are alive, I am alive, we are together, and everything else is replaceable."

Lina was often exhausted after school so rather than cook a meal she and Rosanna would climb fruit trees and live off fruit. They imagined themselves birds, and would take turns at being 28 parrots, rosellas, red-tailed black cockatoos, blue fairy wrens, robin red breasts or willie wagtails. This was freedom and childhood joy rolled into the country they was fast becoming part of their blood. They now always spoke English at home much to their father's frustration when he tried to join in their conversations. "You sound like Greeks," he would jokingly laugh…then they would all burst into Sicilian dialect together. Lina was always healthy and robust like her mother, but Rosanna was more delicate and one day went down with a terrible fever, followed by convulsions and unconsciousness. She was taken nine miles to the Donnybrook doctor, by her father in their horse and cart. The doctor ordered her immediate transfer to Princess Margaret hospital in Perth, which required them to take her by train to Perth, a journey of over four hours. Alfio's heart was distraught as he carried his limp, unconscious daughter into the train for the journey to Perth. He wept because he could never replace the tender loving care of her mother in her life. So often he would say to Rosanna and Lina, "I love you with all of a father's love but it can never be as great as your mother's love." Now Rosanna was facing a life and death matter and he sensed that had she had her mother's care she would never become so ill. The ambulance would be at Perth station to meet the train. Alfio feared that perhaps he would lose Rosanna too. He held her gently knowing how precious and how fragile human life could be and prayed silent prayers. He was not a church man but he knew God in his heart. He often said to Lina and Rosanna, "God lives in our deeds and our hearts." Lina prayed too again, to Mary for help, as she had when her mother died. Her dearest sister, her best friend and help mate, Rosanna…she could not imagine life without her so she prayed fervently to Mary, the Angels, Jesus and every saint she could think about. Rosanna's condition was critical and they were told if she survived the surgery, her recovery would be six to eight months in hospital. The heavens answered Lina's prayers and Rosanna survived but six long months without her sister was heart breaking for Lina. Then one day a letter arrived from Rosanna saying, she was well enough to go home. It was now four months into her hospital stay. Therefore, Lina and her father trained to Perth to bring Rosanna home only to be told she was far from 'all clear'. Rosanna explained to Lina, that she had written the letter because one of the nurses had yelled at her and told her she was a bad child and she had not done anything wrong. She had tried very hard during her hospital stay to be very good and never make a fuss. Anyone who knew Rosanna knew that she was a quiet, delicate, shy and self-effacing child. "I need to have some love," she said to Lina, "so that is why I wrote to you and Dad because I knew you loved me and would come and take me home…I am so lonely." Lina explained this to the hospital and then a hospital visitor was appointed to visit her regularly. On her eight birthday, the hospital staff made her a cake, and the staff bought her a doll and bassinet, the only doll she had ever possessed. Lina was delighted when Rosanna was finally well enough to come home and she promised never to become cross with her for not completing jobs at home again or for 'distracting her when she was trying to read or paint'.

Alfio was very aware of the responsibility of raising these two young daughters as well as providing a living for them all. Without Maria, he sometimes felt as if his right arm had been amputated. He could never really fulfil her role in their lives and bring them into womanhood as a mother could. He honoured women whom he believed a man should protect. Many times he shook his head in disbelief and anguish when a neighbour's children and wife would come and hide in their orchard or the nearby forest because the husband and father was so violent towards them. He regularly said to his daughters, "A man must never hit a woman, it is the ultimate act of cowardice. Never allow a man to hit you. A man who hits a woman is not worthy of her." He believed profoundly in the dignity of human beings and violence was anathema to his world. "A man who hits a woman degrades himself by his violence against a woman who should be protected because she is physically weaker." Violence in the family destroys human health, happiness, livelihood and most of human dignity and integrity. Alfio was a humanist, a God loving humanist who lived his life with goodness as his light. God lived in his heart, in his hands and in his deeds.

Lina's move towards womanhood at 13 years was a difficult transition. One of the neighbours whom her father trusted had started to sexually harass Lina. She was horrified but had nowhere to hide. He would forcibly catch and take her on his horse and cart, and harass her. She was repulsed by him as was Rosanna but his focus was on Lina. They confided in an older friend who said she was powerless to help them. Rosanna and Lina discussed telling their father but they were frightened of any more shooting in their lives. As if to confirm their fears, this neighbour came and shot their cat one day just to show them what power he had. Lina and Rosanna decided to remain silent. Their father had always said that he would kill anyone who touched them and they had seen enough killing in their short lives. Lina particularly worried when her father stayed away guarding the tomato crop in the evenings to prevent kangaroo and emu damage, and they were left home alone because the door of their old house did not lock properly. She lived in fear of a night visit, which never happened, but the fear remained in her body for decades. She became distrustful of men and their underlying sexual motives, except her father whom she sanctified. Relief came two years later when her father purchased what was the most magnificent orchard and house some five miles away from the ten-acre property. Here, they lived in a mansion, a beautiful house with all the conveniences of the time and well way from the sexually harassing neighbour. At last peace had come.

Lina's transition into womanhood was a lonely journey without her mother Maria's guidance and understanding. One day when she was 13 years she awoke and was bleeding profusely, so much so that she thought she was dying. Her father was already at work so she walked to her sister Elena who helped her through her first menstruation and cared for her as she flooded badly. Perhaps it was all the grief of the lost womanhood of her mother, perhaps her body was just made that way but whatever the reason, Lina wept. She rarely ever gave into tears, since her mother had died, but sometimes, the ties of blood are stronger than the will.

Lina had now begun the difficult task of completing her junior certificate by correspondence. She chose to complete, English, Art, Mathematics, Biology and Geography. It was a hard path with little support and Lina remembers studying late at night with just a kerosene lamp for light. She was determined to succeed and the correspondence teacher was encouraging and impressed with the quality of her work. After successfully completing her junior certificate, she was advised by the education department, that in order to complete her leaving certificate, she would have to go to Bunbury Senior High School, the closest high school, 50 miles from her home. The distance was sufficiently great that she would have to board at the convent in Bunbury. Alfio's Sicilian relatives and friends said he was 'mad' to waste money on a girl's education. She would marry soon and it would all be wasted. He would be better to spend the money on a bigger truck to transport his tomato crop. Alfio who had always held firmly to the belief that everyone would realise their human potential. He knew Lina well enough to know that she needed to fulfil her dream of becoming a teacher. His wife Maria, would have agreed wholeheartedly. When eligible, Sicilian young men heard that this now very attractive young woman was about to leave their neighbourhood, offers of marriage came quickly. Lina refused them all, even from the son of the wealthiest landowner. "Lina," her father had reminded her, "he is wealthy and a hard worker, and you will have everything you want, you will never have to work in the fields, your life will be easy. You must think seriously about this."

Lina did think seriously about the offer but refused it, saying to her father, "If I marry, I will never be a teacher, and that is what I want to do."

Alfio took her hand and said, "You have my blessing, Lina, you will be a great teacher, you will bring joy and happiness to many. I will support you all of the way. I understand you must realise your dream." Alfio, as was his nature with his daughters, gave advice but blessed whatever decision they made. He valued freedom, had travelled a long way from his fatherland to ensure his daughters lived and grew in freedom, so he accepted her decision wholeheartedly. Alfio stood head and shoulders above the other Sicilian male migrants in his region, not because of wealth, many were much wealthier than he was, but because of the nature of his character. Without doubt he was a humanist believing in human dignity, the importance of individual freedom to realise one's unique human potential. God was the guiding light within his human soul, ruling his conscience, and defining his integrity. He valued education although poverty ensured that he only had two years of formal schooling, and he appreciated the arts although he never afforded time or money to spend on them. He prized beauty although he had lost so much of it with Maria's death. He strove ethically every day of his life to treat human beings with dignity and respect. Although his own beloved Maria had been murdered in hatred, he did not allow his being to be contaminated by such hatred or revenge.

Chapter 4
Teaching Peace: Enemy Alien No. 72

Alfio reflected with consternation on the state of Sicily. He heard very bad reports from relatives in Sicily. Mussolini's fascist armies were focused on spending money on colonising North African countries while the majority of Sicilians continued to live in dire poverty. Sicilians knew from relatives who were working in the colonies that roads in the conquered countries of Somalia, Eritrea and Libya were better than the donkey tracks still dominating the transport system in Sicily. Sicilian workers earned more in these colonies than at home. Alfio was sceptical of politicians. He sensed their inauthenticity. He would say to Lina, "Much talk by Mussolini and the fascists on making Italy great again, but more suffering and poverty for the people of Sicily." Alfio, whose origins were Greek-Sicilian mused on how Plato would have despaired again at trying to inculcate the virtues of the 'philosopher-king' into the rulership in Rome. He had already tried to teach the rulers in Syracuse many centuries ago with little success. These were the virtues Alfio admired, wisdom in leadership that does not lead to wars but to peace making, wisdom built on the foundation of the core human virtues of justice, truth, beauty and goodness. He was platonic in his very heart, whether or not he knew it. He often said to Lina, "War mongering leaders should fight out amongst themselves their disputes if they cannot settle them by peaceful means. It is a grave travesty of justice that innocent civilians are embroiled in conflicts in which they have no part, nor no interest."

On a family level, correspondence with Maria's sister, Lucia's husband was also concerning. Maria's sister Lucia, a kind, gentle one, grief stricken by the loss of her sister Maria, her mother's madness and her brother's suicide, died of cancer in 1937 leaving five children, one aged two. Even with the help of his servants, her husband was concerned about the future of his children because as head of the 'Cabinari', he could see the inevitable war clouds gathering. What would happen to his children if he died in this war? They were still so young. Thank God, Alfio re-assured himself, that he and his daughters were out of reach of this imminent fascist war but he sympathised with his brother-in-law, caught in the midst of another portending war and grieving the death of his beloved wife Lucia who had borne 11 children for him, including three sets of twins who had died at birth. Lucia's children had always corresponded with his daughters since leaving Sicily, as they had played together in childhood and he had encouraged this, as this was their only link with their mother's family.

Alfio was shocked when Lina, then completing her final year of school in 1939, told her father that Australia was at war with Mussolini and Hitler. He had always thought Australia was too far away from Europe to be involved in a fascist war. Worse news was to follow when Lina informed him that they now both declared 'enemy aliens' and subject to the new Enemy Alien Control Act by the Federal government of Australia. Overnight, they were no longer free citizens. Lina dutifully reported to the nearest police station in October 1939, to collect their enemy alien pass cards, which in effect controlled their every movement out of their home. For Alfio, who had travelled so far to Australia, a journey that had cost him his beloved wife, to protect his family from such control, this was devastating news. He was now part of the Italian community and under police surveillance. His truck for transporting tomatoes and potatoes to Perth was confiscated for the war effort without compensation so they lost considerable money being unable to transport their crops to markets. Prices for potatoes dived as they were dumped again in the sea off the Bunbury jetty because there were no markets for this produce. All guns of the Italian farmers were removed and he worried how he would prevent the kangaroos and emus from destroying the fruit and vegetable crops. They were not permitted radios or any form of communication and their mail was censored.

One night the Sicilian neighbours gathered together to celebrate someone's birthday party and they were all arrested and sentenced to forced labour camps away from their homes and families as authorities argued that they were celebrating a victory of Mussolini. Alfio mused on the ironies of fate. This was like living in fascist Sicily, where people gathering together socially risked random arrest and imprisonment, where their human rights were taken away and they lived in fear and terror for their lives, and their livelihoods were stripped away. He heard of terrible atrocities in the forced labour camps for the Italian farmers in Australia. Unarmed Italian internees were shot in the back by guards as a result of misunderstanding a language command because they did not speak English. The stresses of living away from their families in prison conditions for an indefinite time was sufficient to drive some of the interned men mad. Several returned from internment camps mentally unable to cope with day to day life. It was a tragedy for these Sicilians who had travelled so far to escape the political oppression and economic exploitation of Mussolini's government. Alfio wondered how far a man has to travel to escape this fascist behaviour that denies individual rights at a whim, that shoots people without trial and without charges and which is not accountable to any justice system. Alfio knew he must be very careful being one of the few men left in his district. He could not afford to be interned because he was still responsible for his two daughters. There was no mother to keep the home going. He hardly ever left the farm except for the occasional shopping and became a self-made prisoner on his own farm. No one could accuse him of engaging in any social activities and imprison him. He had already learned the cost of this social control in Mussolini's Sicily and he was familiar with this type of fascist control over the lives of innocent people. Lina could no longer speak to him in a shop or a public street as they were prohibited from speaking Italian in public and he had not had time to learn English. When they went shopping, it had to be in sign language with Lina. He was fortunate to have a fine mathematical mind so that he could review an order and a bill accurately. However, it seared his soul to remember the look in Lina's eyes as she dropped her head down and stared at the pavement when they passed in the public street in Donnybrook. She could not greet him in Italian, the only language he knew. He could see the shame in her eyes and it scoured his soul because they were not people who lived in shame. They were people who lived in integrity and held their head high. How would Lina survive this assault at such a delicate age? He needed her to regularly ask the police officer for permission to have his gun back for a night to shoot kangaroos and emus that were out of hand trampling and destroying his crops. Lina would politely plead to the Donnybrook police officer for permission to sign out her father's gun for the night. He would glower at her and reply, "So you think you are going to be a teacher. We don't want 'dagos' like you teaching our children. Go home to where you came from." Lina did not reply, she hung her head in shame and confusion. How could she tell this man that Australia was her home; that her old home was gone and her mother had died in the process of coming to Australia. One day, the police sergeant tormented her, "So why are you wasting your time studying to become a teacher? They will never let you teach our children. You are the enemy."

Lina simply replied with the fortitude of one who has survived hardship but whose spirit is not broken, "I can only try, that is all I can do."

Try she did, and with all the grit and determination of generations of Sicilians inured by unending invasions, earthquakes, floods and famines. You have to keep going forward because that which is behind you is not a place of retreat. She completed her year 12 leaving certificate in the air raid shelters in the grounds of Bunbury Senior High school in 1939. While attending high school, she applied for Australian citizenship for herself, now 18 years old, and her father. Her application was refused on the grounds that they were from Italy and declared 'enemy aliens'.

In 1940, in order to gain entry to Claremont teacher's college, she was to spend one year as a monitor working for little money as a teacher assistant to other teachers. While waiting for an appointment, the Reverend Mother at the Bunbury Catholic primary school employed her teaching class one and two in exchange for music lessons, free board and ten shillings a week. She was also responsible for supervising boarders going shopping and assisting the year seven teacher. Lina's first monitoring appointment was Greenbushes Primary School, which was only 20 miles from her home so she could see her father occasionally. Shortly afterwards, she was transferred to Wagin Primary School to complete her monitorship for that year. She had to obtain a special police pass to travel the ten-hour train trip to Wagin. In Wagin, Lina boarded at the convent and her spiritual connection to Mary was nurtured by the nuns. She was given a white statue of Mary on her birthday to protect her in her life's journey. Mary the Mother of God to whom she had always prayed in times of distress, from the day her mother died, Mary was the mother she called upon most frequently. Lina cherished this statue, which was etched in the fibre of her soul. In 1942, Mary gave her protection and strength to pursue her dream of becoming a teacher and later in her life, her dream of becoming a mother and a wife.

In 1942, she was granted admission to Claremont Teacher's College during which time lectures were held on the grounds of the University of Western Australia. Every day she would have to go to the Nedlands Police Station to get a day pass to attend the university. The police would arrive at the University to check that she was in class. Lina did not give up although her heart burned with the shame and public humiliation that any 21-year-old young woman would experience in being singled out from the group by a police officer. The University professor requested that the police cease their visits stating that Lina was a genuine hardworking student and the police were wasting their resources tracking her. Her friends joked that it was only because she was so beautiful, with a remarkable stylish set of dresses and an attractive appearance that the young police officers wanted to follow her. She had been blessed with her mother's beauty and sense of style and dress and despite her poverty she was a mistress of designing and making dresses according to the latest patterns on a shoestring budget. Her father was awed by her beauty, which poignantly reminded him so much of her mother at that age. Lina did not notice her beauty and her courage. She worried about her safety, whether she too might be imprisoned like other Italians and the fear that one day she might be randomly excluded from her training as part of the Enemy Alien control act.

Lina graduated at the end of 1942 with subject distinctions and as well as having the distinction of becoming the first female Italian migrant to Western Australia to become a school teacher. This was not noted by the examiners, nor did they recognise the remarkable resilience, grit and grace of this young Sicilian woman to become a teacher. They did however note her remarkable artistic giftedness. Her art-folio reflected her remarkable fluency with the forms and colours of the Australian landscape with its unique flora and fauna as well as some extraordinary designs that must have been in her blood, so typical are they of the patterns of Greek and Sicilian Saracen art designs. It was clear to everyone that Lina was a gifted student and would make an excellent teacher. The male graduates were required to do national service as part of the war effort so there were more vacancies for women graduates than usual. Despite the police officer's words ringing in her ears that 'she would never be appointed to teach Australian children because she was the enemy', she waited for an appointment and prayed again to Mary for a miracle. Then a letter arrived giving her an appointment to North Boyanup Primary School , a one teacher town, 30 miles north of her home in Newlands. This school had a long reputation as one of the most troublesome schools in the state. In the teacher's school journal it was called the 'War zone'. The community was at war, family against family. Cows were poisoned, drinking water contaminated, animals pushed onto the road, shot or run down. It was a bitter war that wrought havoc upon the children and the school community. A previous teacher – a man who could not take the stress; after leaving a note to that effect – had committed suicide by jumping off the Bunbury skeleton bridge. The Education Department had been unable to find a teacher willing to go and take over the school. Perhaps the Education Department staff thought the enemy aliens were disposable, or perhaps they saw it as giving Lina an opportunity to teach, which otherwise may have been denied to her. No one will know now why a 21 year old, first-year out, young woman was appointed to such a direly troubled school. Whatever the reason, Lina had been underestimated. They did not know that she knew more about family wars than most people. They did not realise that she had learned to survive and to tread lightly on the earth. They did not know the calibre of a young woman bred on beauty, integrity, goodness, honesty, tolerance and forgiveness in a world marred by hatred, violence, poverty, greed and discrimination.

Lina was exactly the right teacher for the community. The students were speechless the day she arrived, and described their initial impression, "We thought this most beautiful woman had just arrived from Hollywood to teach us." Lina employed all her strategic experience in family feuding and immediately made it clear to all parents of all the students that she would be unable to attend any homes for meals or visits, as she was very busy in the evenings preparing for class the following day. On weekends, she would ride her bicycle the 30 miles home to Newlands to assist her elderly father with the housework. The parents accepted this rationale and Lina now applied every effort to engage the children to create an environment of beauty, goodness and tolerance as she had a strong allegiance to Plato's model of education. Children become what they are exposed to, so children's education should be dominated by images of the great virtues of goodness, honesty, beauty and truth. Lina made this a reality. With few resources, she used her artistic creativity to create a classroom populated not just by the children but also by all the beautiful birds and flowers that surrounded the school. She created outlines for these and the children coloured, painted, and recycled paper to create their forms on the classroom walls. Using mud from the creek they made three tiered cakes and had school parties together munching on potatoes baked in the coals brought from her father's farm. She created plays, fancy dress balls and made all the costumes from paper painted and coloured. Peace descended in the playground because the children were so occupied creating that there was no time for fights. As parents saw the transformation of the classroom and the change in their children's attitude to school attendance, the light shed by this teacher touched them also. The inspector gave Lina an A grade teaching report and he was particularly pleased with the craft work, the felt toys the children had created, brooches made from bread dough and painted macaroni necklaces dyed and coloured, shopping bags made out of sugar bags with native birds embroidered on them with wool, to name a few of Lina's creative class activities. Now she breathed with the Australian landscape, its birds, animals and flowers a feature in all her art and craft work with the children. She had the children form a bird club and note down every bird they saw and draw them or paint them and write about their habitat. They lived in a landscape through which she enlivened the classroom, awoke in their young hearts, and minds the beauty of it all. For the children it was a longed for escape from the drudgery of milking cows, or rounding up sheep, the repetitive daily grind of their existence. Into their lives, she brought colour and joy, laughter and kindness. Poverty was rife among these dairy communities, few of the children had shoes and many were scantily clad during the winter months. When she could, she provided the children with baked potatoes or a roast rabbit cooked in coals outside the classroom. Around the school house, she taught the children how to garden, to grow flowers and vegetables, to tend to their garden plots, and to mend clothes. She had survived poverty and rural isolation and she knew in her blood the antidotes that nature so abundantly provided. In her spare time, she embroidered exquisite table cloths with patterns of bottlebrushes and gum flowers that she designed. There was only khaki material available and red, green, brown and yellow cottons as these were the colours required for military uniforms. Lina breathed beauty into these colours with the forms of the Australian flora and the finished products were exquisite. There were no angels on the ceiling to fresco in her crochet work as her mother would have crocheted in Sicily, but here the land in which she lived and taught, became her shrine and her tabernacle for beauty.

No one remembered that she was an enemy alien, except the local police who dutifully wrote out a pass for her every morning at the police station then checked in at the one teacher school to make certain she was where she said she would be. Lina felt deeply shamed by it all and it carved into her sensitive soul. One weekend, when sharing her feelings of distress and shame with her sister, Rosanna, who was completing high school, Rosanna laughed, "I would just tell the children that he is my boyfriend and just cannot keep away from me." Rosanna had also completed her teacher training by the end of 1943 and was appointed to the town of Collie. Her father was now alone on the farm as his two beautiful youngest daughters had realised their ambition to become teachers and his two oldest daughters were now busily occupied with children and farm work.

Lina's gratitude and loyalty to her father and the sacrifices she knew he had made on their behalf was never forgotten. While at the North Boyanup Primary school, she would ride 30 miles home on her solid rubber-tyred bicycle on rough gravel roads to see her father and clean his house. This was her weekend routine. She knew he not only provided for her materially to realise her dream of becoming a teacher, but that he had given her even greater gifts. He had taught her the values of honesty, goodness, integrity, the value of beauty and justice and truth, freedom, and she knew in her heart that he had shaped the quality of her heart and mind so that she could shine her light in the world. Therefore, she would make sure that she only brought him happiness and joy. In 1945, her application for Australian citizenship and that of her father's was re-instituted, and they were declared Australia citizens. Freedom at last as she returned their enemy alien passes to the police station and reclaimed their radio and her father's gun. Australia had been her home for most of her life and at last Lina had written evidence that she was formally recognised as Australian. They had to renounce their Italian citizenship and to formally accept the offer of Australian citizenship. Rosanna had married an Australian so had automatically been granted Australian citizenship through marriage.

In 1946, now an Australian citizen, Lina was transferred to Rocky Rise near Wagin, another one teacher school, where again she inspired the students with her goodness, beauty and artistry. As in so many one teacher schools, she was the teacher, nurse, cook and carer. Lina taught the children reading, writing, art, craft, gardening, de-loused their hair with kerosene before school when necessary, created fires for cooking basic wild food like rabbits to feed them and had the children grow vegetables for the school to supplement their lunches. To brighten the school yard they planted red and white carnations. The following year, Lina was transferred to Muntadgin despite parent protests to the education department to keep their school open. Lina continued to create successful classrooms that inspired children and parents alike. They were artistic environments where nature, beauty, and the creative arts were core to the children's learning. However, despite her successes, Lucy became concerned for her father, Alfio. It was a three day train trip home to Newlands and three days return trip with only one week's holiday between terms, it was becoming very challenging to keep regular contact with her father. Lucia's health, normally robust, had also had been challenged when she passed kidney stones, thought traditionally to be the result of deep-seated fear. She applied for a transfer close to Newlands and was appointed to Goodwood Road School in 1948, which meant she could ride her bike home every weekend and care for her father cleaning the house, cooking him meals and listening to his reminiscences of Sicily and of her mother. So often he would tell Lina, "She was a wonderful wife and mother. She will always live in my heart." He never told her that she was so like Maria that she brought him great joy and sadness simultaneously when he saw her. Rosanna knew though, she would say to Lina, "Dad sees our mother too when you visit him." Lina could see that he was aging fast and now had a very lonely life. Knowing how much of his life he had devoted to her and her sister, she vowed she would make his care a priority for her life. Wherever she was appointed to teach, she returned for all her holidays to take care of her father. Alfio knew in the depths of his heart that she would never marry, while he was alone and alive. He knew that her loyalty and love would over-ride all else. He and Lina had survived many tragedies and hard times together and this had created a profound bond that, while understandable, had to be loosened so that Lina could move on and have her own family life and not just become his carer. He knew that as much as Lina loved teaching, she also wanted to have her own children and a family. For many days and weeks, he wrestled with his dilemma. There was no space in his heart for any woman but his beloved Maria. He had never even thought of another woman because he still breathed her scent, her warmth and her love even after these many years of her death. However, he reasoned that in order to set Lina free to have her own family life, he must re-marry. It did not need to be a love match, it could not be a love match because in his heart, Maria still lived. Simply a companion woman who would take care of his physical day-to-day needs. He would treat her with kindness and respect, and provide for her materially. Via relatives in Sicily, a 41-year-old, unmarried woman was recommended to him named Donnella. When she arrived, he was 72 years of age. It was 1951 and Lina was teaching in Duranillin. She was now 30 years old and even the school inspector was suggesting that it was time she married. Alfio told Lina of his portending marriage with Donnella, explaining to her that she was not a replacement for his beloved Maria but a companion in his aging years so that Lina would be relieved from feeling the need to care for him. Lina understood but her oldest sister's husband was very critical, claiming that he was far too old to remarry and that he would squander his estate through such a marriage, feeling directly affected as a beneficiary to his will. Marina, Lina's sister, always quiet and compliant stood by her husband as was the custom in those days. Lina, Rosanna and Elena supported their father's marriage and so it came to pass. Donnella arrived and the arrangement with Alfio worked well. Again he had a woman in his house, a wife and domestic life ran quietly. They were both surprised to discover the following year that she was pregnant. Alfio revised his Will ensuring that Donnella would inherit a house in Perth city and a large sum of money would be set aside for the child to inherit upon turning 21 years of age. Alfio also altered his will to exclude from inheritance his oldest daughter as her husband had refused to speak to him or allow his wife to speak to him following his marriage to Donnella. Alfio was not a vindictive man, but ingratitude was not an insult he bore lightly.

The sole link between Lina and Alfio remained strong despite the fact that Lina now visited less often and worried less, knowing her father was in Donnella's care. While teaching in Culbin, in 1952, Lina had a dreadful premonition and dream on a Thursday night. In the dream, her father was very ill and she was holding him in her arms. He was struggling to breathe and holding his heart as if in great pain. She received a telegram the next day telling her that her father was gravely ill, and had experienced a heart attack that previous night at the time at which she awoke holding him in her arms. It was unlikely he would live long. Lina took a leave of absence to visit him and knew when she saw him that his life was running out. He died a few weeks later, during the August school holidays, with Lina and Donnella by his side. For Lina, the grief was unspeakable. She undertook all her family responsibilities of organising the funeral, and ensuring that his estate was passed to the executor. Lina dutifully completed all the paper work for the family and wept silently as she had done at her mother's death. She fervently prayed to Mary again and hoped that he was at last united with her mother for he had been such a good father, a wise and honest man. The local bank manager gave the eulogy describing Alfio as 'the man with the whitest soul who had ever lived in the district'. His life was un-notable in many ways, but his resolute character was inspirational and his strong spiritual humanistic values profoundly shaped Lina's life.

He was buried in a simple grave, 10,000 kilometres from his beloved village of Fiori near Monterosso in the forest cemetery at Donnybrook where dozens of pioneering Sicilian migrants are laid to rest. Lina designed the headstone. Pure white marble, with a simple cross, and vine leaves frescoed behind the cross, symbol of his love for her, his family, Maria and his beloved Sicily. As his coffin was lowered into the ground, Lina died too. No one would ever call her Lina again. From that day forward, Lina would never hear the music of her Sicilian name "Lina" again, nor hear the voices of her ancestors call her name. Lina was now Lucy, whose roots no longer grew in the fertile soils of the chestnut groves on the slopes of Mt Etna, but whose life was rooted in the vast wheat belt country of Western Australia. There were no cyclamens here to gather, only endless stretches of golden wheat and flowering gums, from time to time, whose blossoms savaged by the cockatoos were spread over the earth like confetti.

Chapter 5
A Marriage Truce

In 1953, Lucy arrived in Kondinin, one of the remote eastern wheatbelt towns in Western Australia, in fact one of the towns east of the rabbit proof fence. The red earth was striking against the stark blue skies and the straggly white-barked gum trees forced their scantily clad branches into the searing heat while defying the burning sun with their twisted dance. As Lucy walked down the main street, her attention was taken by the beautiful display of gladioli flowers in the Butcher's shop. Lucy loved flowers and each day she would walk past the butcher's shop to admire the varied flowers displayed there, roses, stocks, dahlias, carnations, daffodils. Here was an oasis of European flowers in a desert of scrub flowers. The butcher was new to town too. In a strange quirk of fate, they both boarded at the Kondinin Hotel, being the only accommodation in this little outback town. Lucy, now 32, was the belle of the town with her array of beautiful stylish dresses, haute couture for such a little country town and the envy of all the women. She was the teacher of years 1 and 2 at the local primary school and much admired by the children and their parents. She brought her usual passion and enthusiasm to the class and transformed it from what had been described as 'a bunch of unruly country children' to keen students engaged in a range of educational hands-on projects from gardening, arts, crafts and sewing. She did not go unnoticed by the new butcher, Len, who met her during one of the local dinner parties and professed his love for her as they walked back to the hotel together. It was not long before they were engaged to be married. Len was 39 years of age, an Irish Catholic, and veteran of the Second World War having fought in the Middle East and in New Guinea in the 7th/2nd division of the 9th battalion. Len had been noted for his lightening quick reactions that had saved many a 'mate' from death. He had been awarded the oak leaf for bravery and, ironically, he wrote volumes of poetry while on the battle front. He battled the war mongering demons of nationalism versus his profound sense of the need for peace. After the battle at El Alamein, when he was sent to collect the German soldiers' guns, any allegiance to nationalism was blown away when he noticed that their guns were manufactured by the same company as his own battalion's guns. After that, Len fought only to survive and save his mates' lives. In the quagmires of Kokodo Trail, where every step was etched in the blood of his mates, he was wounded but he kept fighting and survived for the days of peace that he reminded himself would come. So he returned to Australia, long ago divorced from his first marriage with only the longing for the restoration of peace and beauty in his life. Lucy became the vision materialised. He was passionately in love with Lucy who had never demonstrated any affection to any suitor or potential lover previously but had dismissed them all in the pursuit of her own career. She was beautiful, stylish, hardworking and loyal, but he did not know that her warmth, passion and joy had died with her mother. When Len proposed to her, she said, "Yes," not because her heart was beating wildly, or she was overcome with desire. Lucy rationalised the marriage offer and decided that at 32 years of age, it was essential she marry if she were to have children. She was impressed by Len's charm, style and devotion to her, as well as the beauty and cleanliness of his shop. At the end of the year, Lucy was transferred many miles away from Kondinin to Mount Many peaks. This town was east of Esperance and overlooked the wild southern ocean. There she was to open the new school as headmistress. They set their wedding date for 22 May 1954 and Len wrote many passionate love letters to Lucy during the five months that they were separated by this considerable distance. Lucy's responses were always very logical but somewhat cool. Either

Len did not notice the gap between his warm effusive passionate letters and her logical cool responses or perhaps he hoped it would change with time.

Deeply in love, he bought a family home for them to start their new life as a married couple in Kondinin. As was departmental policy in those days, Lucy was forced to resign as a teacher. Lucy was pregnant almost immediately and I was born nine and half months later on a hot March day when the temperature exceeded 44 degrees centigrade. It was a difficult birth requiring forceps but both my mother and father were delighted to have a daughter. Fortunately, unlike many of my peers, I had no missing limbs as my mother, Lucy had decided not to take the thalidomide tablets prescribed for morning sickness and had left the jar unopened on the shelf. This was the Sicilian method of taking medication. For generations without doctors, Sicilians thrived through hard work, sleep and good food. Only the hardy survived, so illness was usually short lived and transitory. Medications, except for herbal remedies, were never available

My mother, Lucy, coped with the traumas of her childhood through hard work, diligence, routine and reason. It was to be expected that I was raised like clockwork on four hourly routines and my mother boasted that by four months I could feed myself with a bottle propped up on a pillow. She busied herself with my father's butcher shop and his son Terri from his first marriage, who was serving an apprenticeship there and living with us. Cleaning, washing, cooking, growing vegetables, caring for my father and me, meticulously, was not entirely satisfying for Lucy. She leapt at the opportunity to return to teaching when the school suddenly lost a teacher and was desperate for a relief teacher. The school was happy for her to take me with her to class. My father, blinded by the convention of the day, and the pride that he could support his family, was furious when he heard the news and threatened to take me to the butcher shop with him if my mother accepted the offer. Lucy uncharacteristically capitulated and tried to throw herself into the community. She joined the mother's groups, assisted with the church cleaning rosters, and made many female friends who also had children. Then, when I was twelve months old, she found out that she was pregnant again. This was not a welcome pregnancy. Too soon for my mother after my difficult birth. Tensions and conflicts with Len were becoming commonplace. She was very critical with high standards of perfection, which she placed upon herself and everyone else, and my father found it increasingly attractive to spend time after work with his mates at the pub. This infuriated my mother who did not come from a cultural background where men drank excessively in groups. A glass of wine with the meal was normal for her, but two to five hours at the pub after work was incomprehensible. She riled against my father because she felt deeply rejected and abandoned. The home was picture perfect, she dressed like a model even during the working day, she worked hard for the business, and could not understand why he did not want to spend all his free time with her. He felt bewildered, rejected, criticised, and increasingly unable to make his new wife happy. Feeling powerless and demeaned, my father would sometimes 'kidnap' me and take me away with him for hours, even while I still a very young baby. This both worried and tormented my mother who never argued or expressed any external anger but withdrew even further into her critical, cold, hard, fortressed world from where she fought her emotional battles against my father.

My brother's birth was a turning point in the relationship. My mother bled uncontrollably and the inexperienced country doctor looked on powerlessly, not certain what to do. She groaned and moaned and the baby remained stuck. Feeling she would bleed to death Lucy asked a friend to call Len to come and help her. He arrived quickly from his workplace and was horrified exclaiming, "I have never seen so much blood even when I kill a bullock." A man of action, he demanded immediate intervention to stop the bleeding or he would call the flying doctor service and have her transferred to Perth. He was a man who did not hesitate to act and act quickly. He had saved many of his comrades' lives during the war by his speedy action and here he saw a fight for life and death again.

As on the battle fields, he did not wait for orders, he took action fast and furiously. He had every medical person available summoned to my mother's bedside to save her life. After many, many injections, and a rugged forceps delivery, my mother survived. Normally so robust and without ill health, she was so weak that she had to be carried home for full bed rest. Len was shocked and the thought of being widowed with two young babies shook him to his foundations. He came home early after work, organised house help to cook and clean while Lucy lay bedridden unable to feed her new-born son. Len did not bond with this child that seemed the cause of so many family problems already and barely a few weeks old. Lucy knew that she had nearly died and did not want her children to be motherless as she relived the pain of losing her own mother. She tried vainly to make the marriage work but was now very reluctant to have any sexual contact for fear of another pregnancy, which she did not feel she would survive. Len realised how precious she was now, but a slow silent wall was building between them, neither knowing how to reach the other person, yet their destinies now inextricably tied together by two children, their love of flowers and their hopes for a life without further death or war.

They no longer shared dreams, talked about their future together, or made any plans. It was as though they lived together but in separate universes. Then came the critical day when Len discovered that his business had gone bankrupt. His son from a previous marriage who was his apprentice had been stealing money to give to his mother and Len could not meet the debts owed to his suppliers. He did not discuss the situation with Lucy. She was shocked to discover one day that he was bankrupt, and the house in which they lived was being sold. Len had a health breakdown, which for him was always an outbreak of ulcers so severe, he had to be hospitalised in Perth. He wrote many letters to her from hospital with suggestions of what they could do together to solve the predicament in which they found themselves. She never replied and the letters from Len were left unanswered. Lucy felt deeply abandoned, her very security shattered and in her cold logical way, she assessed Len as unable to provide a livelihood to support her and her two children. She had nothing to say to him and turned all her energies and resources into survival. With a 12 month old baby and a two and half year old, she single handily packed the house, organised a removal truck to take them the 350 miles to Perth where she rented a small house opposite Hyde park. I remember her anguish well, never expressed outwardly but burning in her eyes and pouring from every cell in her body. It was as though her mother or father had died again. I felt the pain although too young to understand the reason as I watched her nurse my brother in her arms all the way to Perth while she was seated next to the removalist truck driver. I wondered where my father was. My heart sank that he was not at the house when we arrived either. The house was dark, dreary, cold with peeling grey paint, the grey Perth sand lifeless and dead without the colour of the red earth to which I was accustomed and the treeless backyard and flowerless front yard made my little heart sink. I remember the grey picket fence and the dirty children next door who asked me to put my little hand through a hole in the fence and then stole my little emerald ring. I remember the black bats in my bedroom and my mother sitting silently and praying by her bedside that night saying 'Hail Marys'. I did not know as a child that she was deeply worried as to how she would support us. She had just fought off the bailiff who came to repossess all the furniture in her Kondinin home, but she had meticulously kept every receipt and proved that she had purchased every household item with her own money. She approached the Education Department for special dispensation as a married woman to teach on the grounds she was the only breadwinner and was given a temporary position, at half a man's wages as a relief teacher at Bayswater. A strange lady called 'a babysitter' came to take care of my brother and I, but I cried when my mother left because I wanted my father and my mother who was now disappearing each day out of my life. Perhaps, Lucy waited for Len to find us but he did not return. He sent her a note saying that he had been discharged from hospital and joined the army. He was posted to the Eastern States.

I never saw my mother show any feelings or cry. She had stoicism as though she accepted suffering as an inevitable part of her life and the challenge was to keep overcoming life's obstacles while maintaining one's moral core of integrity, honesty and loyalty to one's commitments. I would not say she was impervious to pleasure or pain, joy or sorrow but she managed these with quiet reason and rationality and without any display of emotion. It was as though she had accepted early in her life the burden that fate was offering her. Therefore, although her dream of a peaceful, happy marriage was in pieces, without agitation or passion, she decided very logically that her best option was to go it alone, in an era when women did not go it alone. Her father's estate had endowed her with 2000 pounds, sufficient to purchase 50% of a good suburban house in North Perth. After the banks knocked her back, she pleaded with a building society to lend her the remaining 50%.Despite being a woman and having no permanent employment, it was granted. Perhaps it was the prayers to Mary; perhaps her father's spirit overshadowed her and protected her, but for whatever reason, in 1958, my mother signed off on a hefty mortgage for our new home.

Our new home was only three miles from the CBD, a quarter of an acre with the most magnificent backyard with two big Kurrajong trees that I made my home. The house was well built and I had a beautiful bedroom. The toilet was outside and the laundry too, but that was the design in that era. My mother knew how to manage poverty and with only causal relief work teaching set about creating the best life she could for us. Added to her stoicism was an ethos of hard work derived from her father and mother. I remember within a few weeks of moving to North Perth, barely three years old, holding the kerosene lamp at night for my mother while she planted fruit trees, vines and vegetables for us in this huge backyard. Soon there was a chicken pen and plenty of eggs. I watched with wonder in the evenings and weekends when my mother was not teaching, as she would transform old dresses discarded by the neighbours into beautiful clothes for me. She would carefully unpick them, salvage the good material and create a new design that I could wear. She made us children dressing gowns from old curtains, knitted our jumpers and wasted nothing. I learned during our weekly shopping how to choose the products on special and what to buy to get the 'best value'. I also learned honesty at the same time when I took a little plastic toy attached to the outside of a Weetbix box as a souvenir during one of our shopping trips. I was only four years old but I had to accompany my mother and return it to the shop and apologise to the shopkeeper. I was very ashamed and never did anything like that again because I could feel the burning shame in my mother's heart that I had caused.

My mother had an extraordinary capacity to manage prodigious amounts of activities through time-tabling. As children, our routines were never disrupted. We ate each meal at the same time each day, slept at the appointed time, and assisted with chores of shopping, cleaning and gardening at prescribed times on the same day. It was taken for granted that every child lived an organised routinised life and it gave us a great inner sense of security. We could plan our childhood life so easily because there were few unscheduled events. Little did I realise at the time that my mother's persistent commitment to organisation and predictability, which made my childhood secure, was her defence mechanism against her own fears of further violent trauma in her life. As a child, she had not been able to control the events which led to her mother's murder and her fearful experiences but as an adult, control of her environment could be mastered through organisation, timetabling and routine. This brought her a great sense of wellbeing, security, order and achievement. Our home was always tidy, our clothes always predictably clean on the right days for the right activities and even our holidays were scheduled to the same place each year. One week was spent having the wildest fun on her sister Elena's farm at Newlands and visiting our Sicilian relatives, cousins and aunts who treated us like royalty. They always showered us abundantly with kisses, good food, gifts, and fresh produce to take home. I loved these holidays, climbing the apple trees like a bird, chasing massive flocks of chickens, wading in the creek while my mother chatted in her rusty Sicilian to her beloved older sister Elena. They were so alike, I always thought and had so much to talk about that as a child I was amazed how long they could talk to each other without stopping to eat or drink. My mother adored Elena, often referring to her as Sancta Venerina. She had prayed and performed life-saving miracles on children that the doctors had written off as dying. She was generous, warm and indescribably energetic and I loved her too. Since her mother's death, Elena had been my mother's mother and even in her adult years, she would ring her to garner her wise advice. Then there was always a week at the seaside with her younger sister Rosanna, who regarded my mother as her mother. They were very close to each other and shared their school holidays together for all of my childhood. Both were excellent primary school teachers, artistic, intelligent and kind, but Rosanna lacked my mother's confidence in life, though she was a very gentle soul and relied upon my mother for advice. She painted exquisite oil paintings of Australian birds and animals within the walls of her house as well as on canvasses, played music, sang and also had a most beautifully furnished house. I loved the angel statues above her bed, the shining crystal jewellery and the fine china on her shelves. My childhood was filled with memories of her knitting me beautiful jumpers, making dresses with my mother for me as she did not have a daughter. I always felt closer to her than my mother. We seemed to be kindred spirits and had shared sensitivities in life and I secretly wished, as a child, that she was my mother. Her son, Roger, preferred my mother in childhood and we discussed swapping mothers from time to time. In these childhood wishes, I was certain my father would come with me if I went to live with Rosanna, even though she was happily married.

Often, I wondered if my father would ever return as I sat perched daily on the low brick fence at the front of my house. This was an excellent place to watch the road; to see who was coming up the street and notice which other children in the street were free to play. I would smile sweetly to the women who worked at the lolly factory two houses up the road and they would reward me on their way home with lollies that I was not allowed to have. My mother believed 'sugar causes worms, diabetes, makes you fat and rots your teeth'. At Easter, I was given large solid sugar Easter eggs by the lolly factory women. These beautifully decorated multi-coloured sugar eggs were promptly confiscated by my mother and consigned to the compost heap, while she commented that they were probably bad for the soil as well. Then one day, I did see my father coming up the street. I ran to hug and kiss him, I was so excited. He had finally come home. He hugged me and told me how much he missed me. Mum and Dad did try to make it work again. Dad opened another butcher shop, Mum kept on teaching wherever she could get work. Dad was impressed with our house and the backyard, and soon Dad and Mum were planting wonderful flowers in our front garden. Gladiolas, ranunculus, dahlias to add to the rosebushes Mum had already planted and the patch of carnations that I had planted. Often in evenings as a family we would go for walks either 'window shopping' or just enjoying our neighbour's gardens and the evening air. There was so much freedom as a child. We could roam the neighbourhoods at will, as long as we were home for meals, and in the hot summer evenings we would sleep on the front verandah or the front lawn.

It was not perfectly peaceful. There were arguments, from time to time, although my mother never raised her voice; my father could become quite emotional. He was the fourth child in an Irish Catholic family of 14 children, whose father, a train driver, had done the best he could to support his brood, but at 12 years of age each boy had to leave school, take a swag, and go looking for work. Dad had always had it hard and was used to living with nothing. He had a generous spirit and would give away the coat he was wearing if he found some person in greater need than himself. My mother never understood this behaviour and blamed him for losing his butcher shop business by giving meat away to children whose parents sent them to tell him they were hungry while knowing that he would not refuse meat to children. My father's mother was a buxom, kindly Scottish woman, Ellen, who adored every baby she had borne and was gifted at singing and piano playing. My father adored his mother and so did I, as she was my only surviving grandparent and always greeted me with warmth and affection as though I was a little angel. Dad's father retired to train racehorses and died of a heart attack during a race at Ascot. My father had all the feelings that my mother lacked, and she had all the rational, logical financial abilities that my father lacked. Perhaps if they had celebrated each other's differences, they might have created a harmonious household. My father simply did not understand my mother's fearful violent childhood or understand how to make her happy and she was very critical and spurned his efforts. He proudly came home one day with a sign that said 'St Lucia' which could be placed on the front of the house and my mother coldly asked him to dispose of it as she deliberately hid her Italian identity from everyone. Now married with an Irish name, she was unidentifiable as Italian. Lina had died and Lucy was striving never to be an enemy alien again. On another occasion, my father made a little night light for me with a tiny globe that could be left on above my bed during the night because I suffered from terrible night terrors seeing dark evil forms in the air around me. I would run crying to my parents bed and my mother would coldly order me back to my bedroom and I would cling to my father who would get out of bed and come and sit with me and hold my hand till I went back to sleep. When my mother returned from work and he showed her the little night light he had made, my mother ordered it to be removed. It would use electricity, and as he was not a certified electrician it could prove dangerous. At that moment, my soul was seared by my mother's complete lack of comprehension for my suffering. I went into alliance with my father's warmth and passion. This alliance was fertilised by my mother who rejected my warm passionate nature with comments like 'you are just like your father' with the unspoken subtext of 'not good enough'. My mother often referred to Jack, my brother who was a quiet, unemotional child, as 'just like her' with the subtext of 'has the acceptable and desirable behaviour and character'.

Disaster struck our family, the year I was turning six. I heard my father shouting at my mother while she stood accusingly pointing to red lipstick on his shirt collar. Words were flung about like 'no sex', 'no warmth' and my mother's face became icy white. I watched with horror as my father threw the wedding photo on the mantelpiece, to the floor which shattered into pieces and broke my heart. He hurriedly packed a small suitcase; gave me the only material possession he had, a statue of a happy man holding a beer and left. My mother said it was ugly and I should throw it away but I concealed it under my bed. Then court orders for a 'legal separation' were instituted by my mother who being Catholic did not believe in divorce. My father was granted access on weekends. Sometimes he came and most times he did not. Once we visited a house where another woman lived who was kind enough to my brother and I, but my heart never recovered from the shattered wedding photo moment and I wondered what I had done wrong to cause so much trouble between my parents. Their pain was in my little body, in my blood and in my shattered heart. Each Saturday, I would sit like a sentinel on our front fence waiting for my father. Many times I would wait till my sun clock had moved its shadow across the sky and I was sinking with exhaustion and despair into the horizon. I would know then that my father was not coming. I would wander in sorrow to dinner only to hear my mother repetitively pronounce, "What can you expect from an alcoholic, a no hoper. If it were left to your father, we would all be living in tents in the street." While rationally, I knew this was true, my heart had another story, a story of delight in my father's warm arms, joy in his wisdom as he read me poems; piggy backed me around the yard and shared stories about the stars in the night sky.

If only Lucy and Len had understood that they were both refugees of war, acknowledged and accepted each other's wounds, they may have found peace together. Len never really understood the extent of my mother's fear, that her frozenness was from the terror of having witnessed the murder of her mother, nor did she tell him of this tragedy. He did not know about her sexual abuse as a girl, her fear of dying in childbirth and leaving her children motherless, so it was impossible for him to understand why she was so resistant to having sex. He did not understand her middle class commitment to working hard and saving hard to accrue property. He had always lived with little as he grew up in profound poverty but with warmth and love. He had survived by his wits, alone since 12 years of age working outback stations, living in tents with campfires and meagre rations. His older brother drove cattle through the Canning Stock route, the heart of the Australian deserts from Wiluna in the south to Wyndham in the north. He followed him or else had dreams of finding gold and spent years prospecting in Leonora, Menzies and Mt Magnet. He voluntarily went to war in 1939 as it was his first secure job, like so many men around him who had lived in dire poverty through the depression. A sensitive but quick-witted man, he had survived the El Alamein campaign in the Sinai Desert, survived being shipped back to Fremantle to defend Australia from the Japanese invasion. It was a four-week drive in cattle trucks across this vast country, its desert and its pastures till, finally, the troops arrived at Atherton near Cairns to experience for the first time the tropical rainforests. He fought the bloody Kokodo Trail campaign in New Guinea. He saw sights and sounds, suffering of his mates that no human being should ever have to witness. He survived and returned with amoebic dysentery, gunshot pellets still lodged in his belly and mentally savaged. He had enjoyed a beer or so before the war but now alcohol was his drug of choice to block out the horrifying images that would recur in his mind at random times during the day and the night. Marriage to my mother, so beautiful, so pure had seemed a way to block out this torment, but of course she had her warring torments too, perhaps more deeply concealed, and together they were torment for each other's fears and insecurities.

Lucy focused on being a good mother and an excellent teacher, now that her dreams of a happy family had crumbled into dust, while Len joined the work crew building the Trans-Australian Railway across the Nullarbor Plain. It was away from all alcohol, and he found peace in the great vastness of the Australian deserts, landscapes and night skies. I missed him profoundly and my mother always a person to do the 'right thing' insisted we write to him fortnightly and keep him informed of our activities, as the train crews only returned at Christmas time for a couple of weeks. I had a passionate delight in my father's letters. He wrote to me about the stars, the great Southern Cross, the saucepan in the sky, Orion's belt and told me about the songs he sang by the night fires in the desert as he played guitar and violin. He posted me bunches of pink and white everlasting daisies gathered from the desert fringes, he sent me the most beautiful huge maroon and golden beetle that killed itself accidentally hitting the window of his railway carriage where he lived. I received treasure from the great red-golden desert that made my heart sing: boxes of sandal wood nuts, exquisite bird feathers, little coloured rocks…all of which I treasured. I found a beautiful discarded biscuit tin with pink and gold flowers embossed all over it and I regarded it as my treasure box. I placed the feathers and the beetle in it, some desert flowers and other little treasures I had found in the streets. Whenever I was sad or missed my father, I would sit on my bed, take out my treasure box and look at all these beautiful objects that I so loved and which reminded me of my father in the great Nullarbor Desert. One day, my brother and my cousin, Roger, Rosanna's son decided to harass me, so they stole my treasure box, and buried it in our backyard. They would not tell me where they had incarcerated it. I was devastated and wept like a river about to burst its banks. I pleaded with my mother to make them give it back to me but she was busy, annoyed by my emotional outbursts and simply told me, "It is just an old tin full of rubbish, do not make a fuss about such trivialities." Only eight years old, I knew I needed justice for such a travesty and I decided my father would execute it. I was not allowed to write to him about anything that was not good and positive so I decided a secret letter was in order. I wrote a long letter to him telling him of my catastrophe, of my mother's lack of concern as well as telling him how much I cried for him not being at home with me. I found the address 'Widgiemooltha' a remote desert town south of Kalgoorlie and I addressed it with much effort. I disappeared down the street, found some discarded glass cool drink bottles, which I deposited at the local shop in exchange for a stamp. Justice was done, a quick reply from my father telling me that the boys would get a 'hiding' when he returned and be forced to find the buried treasure box. He included a ten pound note in it for me to replace my treasures, which was half of my mother's weekly wage at the time. Justice had been done but my mother was not impressed and I was scolded for having worried my father unnecessarily. I was alienated by my mother's logical analysis of my problems as though she had a bypass of my heart. Having been dux in class 1 and 2, that year in class 3, when my father was working all year in the desert, I began to fail. I only remember feeling desolate and grief stricken, and when the teacher wrote on the board, I could only see clouds, white and fluffy. I cheated all year off the boy sitting next to me because I could not think any more. It was as if my brain was dying. My mother was horrified at my appalling school report in which I had failed most subjects and my entire Christmas school holidays were spent on remedial school work, supervised by my mother. Education was highly valued by my mother, and her family, and I knew from age six that I was expected to go to University. She attributed much of my father's alcoholism to his lack of education, as he was forced into menial boring jobs when he was capable of so much more. "If you cannot fulfil your potential," she would argue, "you can never really be happy."

The following year, my mother and father decided to try to restore their relationship and our family life. They both tried very hard. My father joined alcoholics anonymous, obtained a factory job nearby, and my mother continued her relief teaching. She bought a family car and I remember a glorious year of family life. Long drives on the weekend to explore bushland surrounding Perth, or to look at wild flowers, which were still a passion of my mothers. Wonderful fireside times with us all sharing poetry and music as I was now playing piano. Henry Lawson and Banjo Patterson being the favourite poets of my father who had a photographic memory so knew all their poems by heart. My love for the bush poets of Australia has always remained in my heart because they were a transfusion from my father's heart to mine. We had the best flower garden in the neighbourhood as Mum and Dad worked together to create magnificent floral displays. My mother was happier, there was more money and I received a Malvern Star bike for Christmas, which my father taught me to ride. Then gradually and almost imperceptibly, relationship rot started attacking their marriage again. There was criticism from my mother, increasing alcohol consumption by my father and he lost his job. It escalated into a major car accident in which my drunken father wrapped himself and the car around a telegraph pole. It was in the newspapers and my mother was mortified and shamed. My father went back to the bush, out beyond Laverton in the central deserts of Australia, to the only physician he knew, prospecting for gold and my mother salvaged the car and her dreams.

Six months later, he returned home a sick man with the ravages of alcohol and chronic cigarette smoking showing its toll. He was now classified as a war soldier TPI (Totally and permanently incapacitated) and was given a war pension. My mother's loyalty came again to the fore and she offered him accommodation at our home yet again. However, the relationship was irretrievably broken. My father slept in the sleep out. He was never permitted into her bedroom again. My mother never had any other lovers or relationships in her entire life. Her loyalty and devotion remained with my father till his death, but now it was only duty that glued the relationship together. For the next eight years, the relationships followed the predictable cycle. My father received his pension cheque and bought large amounts of port wine. He would eat nothing and only drink wine living in the sleep out talking endlessly and inchoately about the horrors of his war experience. The lines between hallucination and trauma fusing and alternating between troubled ramblings and raging torrents of fear and expletives. Today, Len would be labelled a post-traumatic stress survivor, counselled and medicated. In my childhood, my father was his own broken counsellor, alcohol his medication from the hell states of war that haunted his mind, and flowed through the veins of his wounded body. When the wine and pension money ran out, he would eat a little soup and harangue my mother or my brother. After three months of this behaviour, he was usually writhing in pain from his ulcers. Dutifully, Lucy would ring an ambulance and he would be transferred to Hollywood Hospital where he would recuperate for a couple of months. During this time, peace was restored in the household and there was relief for my mother that she no longer had to clean this putrid sleep out or listen to his deranged ramblings and torments. In truth, Lucy was also a post-traumatic stress survivor from the war but she medicated on hard work and rigid routines with little respite. It was a more skilful option for us children and healthier for her survival. Lucy's loyalty and devotion to family meant that weekly on Sunday we visited our father in hospital, always bringing flowers and treats for him. Lucy was committed stoically to doing the right thing. My mother's behaviour to my father remained driven solely by a stoical duty long after they no longer related as lovers. She served him as a wife but she did not love him. I would be sent by my mother to find my drunken father somewhere fallen asleep on the side of the streets that led to our house. It was my job to help him stumble home where she would have prepared special soups and meals for him. He was grateful for her care but the passion and love had been extinguished. They lived in the same house but not together. The only things they shared were the same address, two children, dead dreams and post-traumatic stress disorder, following the wars in their earlier lives.

I fled home at 18 years to the National University on the other side of the country. My brother, who had never been close to my father, pressured my mother to eject him from the house, so they could have peace from his drunken ramblings. She asked him to leave but he was broken, too ill to work and a chronic alcoholic. He had not even the energy to resort to his usual doctor which was to 'go bush' and camp, and work on prospecting for gold, away from the cities and the alcohol. There, he would heal in the quiet sounds of the desert, the still hope of the starlight nights, and the warmth of the campfires that he so loved. Instead, he began living at a cheap Perth hotel where his money was divided between rent and alcohol, and within months he had a massive stroke, was diagnosed with 'Korsakoff's Syndrome', and recognised no one but my mother. He then became a permanent inmate at Lemnos C class hospital for veterans with mental health conditions where he lived for the next 20 years. His long term memory recovered but his short term memory was irrevocably damaged. He recovered enough in those twenty years to also recognise his children, his mother and a few close relatives.

Stoical as ever, Lucy continued to visit her husband for the next 20 years, weekly, and organised with the hospital for him to have day release every Sunday so he could spend the day with her at the home. She cooked him delicious meals, stood up for his rights in hospital and sorted out any medical issues that needed attention. She was his spokesperson 'until death do us part'. He was grateful for these crumbs of relationship. Lucy in turn soothed her conscience and her soul with 'having done her duty'. There was no heart left for either of them to do anything else.

Chapter 6
Communities in War and Peace

During my childhood, my mother, Lucy, was a sentinel for peace in our neighbourhood. She was known as the teacher and revered by the waves of migrant refugees that came to live in our neighbourhood because of her unlimited kindness, compassion and practical help that she offered them. She helped them with all government documents, social security forms, reading and translating to the best of her ability to each of the families that sort her help. I remember the Macedonians I met in the 1970s telling us of the shootings between their border and Greece and seeking solace in Australia because of their fear of another war. My mother must have deeply understood them having endured her own childhood trauma and family escape to Australia from a portending war. I remember them rehearsing for their naturalisation ceremony in our lounge swearing 'allegiance to the queen and all her hairs'. I collapsed into fits of laughter only to cease abruptly when I saw the pain in my mother's eyes and her reproachful looks. When the neighbours departed, I have never forgotten the quiet lecture she gave me on the difficulties of learning a second language combined with the dislocation of leaving all that is familiar to you. Thereafter, I developed a new compassion for Australians of difference. My mother's spirit like her father's humanistic soul supported the dignity of all human beings. As a younger child, my brother and I were quietly reprimanded if we stared at the two adult dwarfs who lived in our street. This was a challenge because they were our height but could do adult things, so we were fascinated by their difference and unusual gait. My mother reminded us that everyone has feelings and staring at people who are different can make them feel inadequate and hurt their feelings. I did not know then that perhaps she was remembering arriving in this country dressed in black and the weeks and months of children staring at her and her sisters and making fun of them. So many things I did not know or in my childhood ignorance lacked understanding and empathy. When she tried to share with me the beauties of Sicily and her early childhood, I dismissed them derogatively, "Sicily cannot be any good or you would not have come here". In my childhood arrogance, I did not naturally show empathy to migrants. It was one of the finest qualities I learned from my mother.

During the post-Vietnam War, thousands of Vietnamese fled and migrated into Western Australia, our street now housed several Vietnamese families, which was our first exposure to the Asian presence in previously 'White Australia'. Again, my mother was their help through endless rounds of paperwork, advice on schooling; tutoring and English to the migrant children. She never accepted money, but her kindness was repaid in spring rolls and wonderful tasting dishes of food from different nationalities. She modelled tolerance as well, explaining to us that although we were Christians and Catholics, we needed to respect the Buddhist or Islamic religions of our neighbours, as you inherit your religion from the country in which you are raised. Being a human being is the most important religion and this is common to us all.

Having lived through discrimination and exclusion as a migrant and 'enemy alien', she was particularly sensitive to this in her teaching. Often she would recount stories of her teaching in the wheatbelt areas in the 1940s and 1950s about the aboriginal children who would come to school, often without food and the meals she would give them. She spoke compassionately of their mothers birthing children under bushes without homes or medical support in their own country. Only one parent had to object and an aboriginal child attending school would be excluded. At Culbin, she was told by previous teachers that the aboriginal children were housed in a separate school building and the teacher had to move from one building to the other. She was relieved to discover that the practice had ceased when she arrived in 1952. My mother always taught us that discrimination leads to war, because in discriminating against another human being we justify treating them lesser and even badly.

During our childhood, she had continuous employment despite being a supply teacher who could not become permanent because she was married. Headmasters wanted her services because her classrooms were always alive with colour and beauty and the children's basic reading and writing skills outperformed other similar cohorts of students. She taught in many schools across the metropolitan area, never owning a car but always finding a way to get there. Her final teaching appointment was to North Perth Junior Primary where she taught year one with fourteen different nationalities of children in a class of 28 students. More than half of the children spoke no English. She set it her goal to teach those children English and compassion for each other as she noticed at playtime the children teased each other based on size, race or colour. She introduced multicultural food days, lessons about different cultures and most of all modelled her humanistic acceptance of all children. One of her dearest recollections was a tiny year one Vietnamese child whom she often had to carry when the class walked long distances to sport or excursions. The little child called Myn would hold my mother's hand and say, "I love you, my teacher, but I wish I was white."

My mother's response was always, "Myn, you are lovely as you are." She taught the culturally diverse children English language, writing and spelling with a patience and success that few other teachers were willing or able to do. I am certain it was because she knew the experience of transitioning into English from another language and culture from the 'inside'. Perhaps more importantly, she taught them understanding and tolerance for each other's differences circumventing the development of a culture of childhood bullying and instead creating a classroom and playground of peace.

My mother, Lucy, in her behaviours both at home and at school lived as a stoic. She believed all human beings should be treated equally and given equal opportunity in an era, long before it had become fashionable. It was inscribed in her being. She had not heard of laws against racial discrimination, or gender equity, nor did she ever have discussions in these veins. Her acceptance of the place of every human being in the world was part of her breathing, like the air that surrounded her and was a taken for granted state of being. My mother's life was lived with a commitment to virtue in classic alignment with the stoical world view were self-control, rationality, fortitude and quiet endurance are a means for overcoming destructive emotions, senseless suffering and tragedy. For my mother, holding a grudge was senseless; failing to forgive another person was mindless, refusing to apologise for some hurt were all unnecessary and futile.

From the smallest child I remember her telling me the story of Pollyanna whose chief characteristic was 'never to let the sun go down on her anger' and always make peace with those with whom one has shared the day. Telling the truth and being honest were also hallmarks of my childhood. No matter what we had done wrong, we were praised for telling the truth and forgiven for the deed. As a small child around five years I was entranced by the beauty of my mother's dressing table with its glass sliding doors concealing magical containers of sparkling jewellery and the fine bone china exquisitely gold and blue etched container that held her most valuable jewellery. I knew I was not to open these glass windows or ever touch what was exposed in its glittering grandeur behind the windows. One day the temptation was just too much, and I slipped quietly into my mother's bedroom when she was gardening and opened the glass window then picked up the exquisite blue and gold fine china container with a little round, gold, knobbed, blue flowered lid. I was so entranced by the diamond ring and sparkling necklace that when I lifted the lid, I accidentally dropped it and it cracked into two pieces. I was horrified and carefully pieced it together and placed it back on the precious container, closed the glass windows and ran away. This was my earliest memory of the struggle to tell the truth, to apologise and to be honest. I could not quite do it, knowing I had already been told not to touch it and I would be in for a quiet talking to about my deeds, so I hid in the lounge behind the couch, as children often do in their shame. Eventually my mother found me behind the couch and I confessed after a long quiet talking to. I saw the sadness in my mother's eyes. It was indelibly etched into my mind, the suffering I had caused. "Do you know," she said, "this was once my mother's. It is one of the only things of her beauty that I still have in my life."

Beauty was also a hallmark of my mother's world view, not in the trite superficial way but in the true Platonic sense. Like her father, she lived her life honouring the eternal transcendent concepts of beauty, justice, truth, equality that were her internal signposts for goodness and for God. When I was nine years of age, my mother was reading Plato's republic to me and explaining the importance of creating an environment of beauty especially for the right education of children. Images that children are exposed to in their education should be images that inspire beauty, goodness, truth, justice and so that these become the building templates of the child's mind. I saw this daily in her actions. Our home always had at least one vase of beautifully arranged flowers, despite our tight budget. My mother designed and made clothing that was elegant and in joyful colours and patterns. On Saturday afternoons we would create beauty out of old glass jars, disused lolly wrappers and she would teach us how to create beautiful crafts or clothes or paintings. Where most people saw the ordinary, my mother saw the potential to create beauty. Her classrooms were likewise pictures of colour and activity focused on the natural forms of flora and fauna in the Australian bush environment that she continued to bring into her urban classrooms. She would draft onto pieces of linen outlines of plants, animal, and birds that I learned to embroider with many coloured threads. Even our meals reflected her sense of symmetry and beauty and she insisted that there must be at least three different colours on the plate orange/red, green and white/brown for proper nutrition of mind and body.

My mother never told us that she loved us, never hugged us or showed any overt emotion but her day to day life was organised to provide for our material needs in the most generous, and beautiful way possible. It was through such deeds that she understood how to express her love. In an environment where money was very limited, she stretched herself further than most parents would have done. We had music and tennis lessons paid from her frugal budget. She tutored on weekends and the money went into a special jar labelled 'Christmas presents' so she could buy us something special for Christmas. Nothing was too much effort to ensure our material needs were met. The house mortgage was paid, the bills covered and a small amount left for treats. In my entire childhood, my mother only went out once, to an end of year dinner with the other teaching staff. The money she would say is better spent on your children. Determined to make up for her tough childhood, she made sure on rainy days we went to school in a taxi so we would not have to sit in wet clothes all day and catch colds as she often did in childhood.

She retained her faith and commitment to us even when in adolescence we were a disappointment to her. At 16, I became vegetarian much to her confusion and frustration because she so enjoyed cooking us meals. In my search for peace and meaning I stopped attending our Catholic church and started exploring different views offered by the theosophical society. This also confused her and alienated her. Despite her fluid interpretation of Catholicism, her allegiance to good deeds rather than alignment with church teachings, her rejection of the church's teachings on birth control and her dismissal of most of the old testament as violent, warlike and revengeful, she seemed surprised that both myself and my brother started to search for meaning outside of Catholicism.

My brother who had always been her 'littlest angel' now began to deeply disappoint her by bringing shame to her life. At 12 years of age, he was expelled from Christian Brothers

College with a group of around six other boys for stealing goods and selling them on. He himself did not commit the act but was found in possession of stolen goods and my mother was deeply mortified when she had to attend the children's court and hear that he was to be placed on a good behaviour bond. Shortly afterwards, he became obsessed with creating explosives. We were given great freedom as children to roam the neighbourhood, as long as we returned for meals. My brother was secretly experimenting in the back shed with chemicals to create explosions and one day blew most of the skin off one of his hands and had to be rushed to hospital for immediate treatment much to my mother's distress. He was placed in psychological counselling services at the high school he attended and it was discovered he was Mensa IQ of 145. My mother's fear of guns and violence following her childhood witnessing of her mother's murder was re-triggered when she found a sawn off shotgun hidden in the house, placed there by my brother. Where or how he came to possess this gun, he would not reveal and my mother feared his behaviour was rapidly spiralling out of control. He left school at 15 years, having failed most subjects. Meanwhile I was studying for my final year exams, duxed the school and received a converted scholarship to University. I too shared my mother's fear around my brother's pre-occupation with explosives and guns. My mother always believed that self-control, reason and fortitude were the means of overcoming destructive emotions, and challenging incidents but here even her normal equanimity was stretched. At 18 years, I could no longer take the tension in the family so fled to the eastern states informing my mother the day before I left much to her grief. Within two months of being at the national University, I married a very violent man, unbeknownst to myself at the time, a member of the mafia and a displaced person who had arrived in Australia as a refugee in the 1950s. My movements were controlled, and I had very little contact with my mother for the next two years. Two years later, I arrived back at home, with my child having been taken by my violent husband to try and re-piece my broken heart and broken life. My mother stood beside me through all the court hearings which ended in defeat as he had guns and threatened to kill the child if I persisted in claiming custody of her and I was intimidated by his threats. My mother with kindness and generosity supported me to re-attend University and finish my degree. Meanwhile my brother had disappeared overseas and married a woman my mother's age and together they worked on a number of solar and electronic inventions. This had not been my mother's plan for either of her children but her stoical approach to her life and her deeply personal belief in the power of Mary to whom she prayed novenas to help her through this crisis kept her healthy and sane. Many persons with lesser resilience, faith and stoicism would not have survived without serious mental and/or physical health breakdowns.

Chapter 7
Family Violence

Lucy's life entered a new phase in 1991. She was 70 years old. Firstly, after 20 years of devoted care to Len through his time at Lemnos hospital, he passed away from pneumonia. His death was sudden. He had had increasing progressive emphysema due to his chronic smoking addiction, 40 cigarettes a day for over 30 years. At 10 am, the hospital rang to say that Len was unwell. He died at 10.20am. Never a man to complain when in pain or physically suffering, his illness had gone unnoticed by hospital staff until 30 minutes before his death. Lucy was shocked, and went into her frozen fear and sadness. Again the seven year old child seemed to be written on her face, again feeling hopeless and lost in the face of death. Lucy was unable to organise the funeral, for she had seen too many family deaths in her life, and her resilience to death had declined. I took responsibility for all of the funeral arrangements. I was distressed to learn from her that two days before his death he had asked when he was coming down to spend time with myself and my partner in our home and my mother had replied that I was too busy to have him. This was not true, but it was typical of my mother's articulation of relationships in terms of chores to be done, time to be allocated, duties to be fulfilled. Now there were no chores or routines to fill the gaping void in her heart. Her husband was gone.

My father's death was closely followed by my brother's return to live in the family home with my mother. His wife had been accidentally killed in hospital when given the wrong drug, and the stable anchor in his life that she provided, disappeared overnight. My brother, Jack despite qualifications in teaching, librarianship and technology, soon became unemployed and quickly squandered the money they had made from inventions and invested in housing units. For several years he had developed a growing relationship with my mother based on her paying his bills and loans to keep a way the debt collector. In 1991, he chose to move home where our mother provided for all of his needs including cooking, washing, paying his bills, cleaning and the like. His resentment towards our mother, Lucy, that had been increasing over the years now escalated into regular verbal and emotional abuse, intimidation and threats. His behaviour became increasingly erratic as he poured chlorine bleach into her water tank, constructed strange pyramids in odd parts of the house and garden, and began showing signs of paranoia towards the world. He requested I support his intended court application for compensation for emotional abuse from my mother towards us as children. Although we had been close as siblings, this severed any remaining relationship. I refused saying it was untrue and that gratitude for what our mother did to provide for us singlehandedly during our childhood was appropriate. Following his failed court proposal for which he could garner no support, he became increasingly aggressive towards my mother and physical violence began. Lucy, schooled not to accept physical violence, rang the family doctor who had him certified and removed to a mental health hospital where he was diagnosed as thought disordered. It was good that my mother demonstrated boundaries and her right to peace but her overriding sense of duty left her feeling guilty. Torn between protecting her own physical wellbeing and supporting her son, she invested all her hard-earned savings in purchasing a home for him where he could live upon his release from the mental health hospital. For the next 15 years, my mother and brother continued a chronic co-dependent cycle. He did not work, did not socialise, did not form any social relationships and continued to live in a world of his own peopled by conspiracies, paranoia and realities not shared by anyone else. However, in terms of day-to-day living he managed to borrow money from my mother to pay his continuing debts. It was often heart-breaking to visit my mother's home and see her living on the bread line while her comfortable superannuation payments were given to my brother. I tried on several occasions to explain to her the co-dependence cycle which she was caught in with my brother that was unhealthy for both of them. She never understood. "He is my son," she would repeat mechanically, "I must look after him. I cannot see him living in the streets and I do not want him living here." It was as though she was prepared to be crucified for some family value of loyalty. It was typical of her stoicism that whatever challenges life threw up, however difficult, she carried them like a cross without hatred or judgment, just grim determination to survive.

Her son, Jack, used and abused her shamelessly. Over the period of the 15 years, the cycle of abuse was repeated three times. He would trash the house she had bought him which would be filled with rubbish and debris and he would then return and squat in her home. She and her sister Rosanna would then labour for weeks to clean the abandoned house, have it repaired and then she would sell it at a loss. His behaviour at her house would then escalate to increased levels of verbal abusive and emotional intimidation so that she would buy him another house in which to live. Her emotional attachment to caring for him was at times noble, at other times truly pathetic. Watching her wait for him to join the family for Christmas dinner, set a place for him then keep it warm in the oven all afternoon was symbolic of her lost dream of the happy family. He rarely came and if he did, it would be late. He would refuse to eat as though on principle on Christmas day, because he knew it tortured her hopes and dreams of the harmonious family life. Again, like the cycle of dysfunction and co-dependence with my father, respite came into her life through the medical services. My brother had further admissions into mental health services. He was admitted following harassing the local police station officers with stories of murders and victims' bodies, which he was certain, he had located in various parts of the city. On another occasion he was admitted for phoning the airport and informing them that energetic interference with their radar system was about to occur. By this stage, he had been identified as 'psychotic' and 'schizophrenic'. He was also clearly hypochondriac, as I counted 1000 packets of prescribed medications in his house while helping my mother to clean it during one of his hospitalisations. She often sighed when she repeated her mantra, "There is a very fine line between a genius and a madman and Jack has slipped over the line." She continued to devote her life energies to supporting her only son, perhaps because she had always deeply cared for him or perhaps because she derived her sense of value, now that she was retired and Len was dead, by caring for her family. She also accepted it as her fate, in some strange deterministic way. When the trauma was too great, she resorted to novenas to the Blessed Mary to help her endure unto the end. It was all too sacrificial for me, like an unnecessary martyrdom. Initially, I chided my mother for this excessive devotion to what I considered amounted to being a doormat for my brother, but to no avail. After ten years, I said nothing.

When Jack was discharged in 2006, he had not worked for over 20 years and was now eligible for disability pension but he continued to harass our mother for money. Lucy was heartbroken when her engagement ring disappeared from her wardrobe, the only item of real value she had ever owned, after a visit from my brother to her home. He had begun to develop fantasies about the family diamond mines in South Africa and about my father's role with the Secret service intelligence systems in Germany during the Second World War. To all of these my mother listened patiently. In between these fantasies he used and abused her either passively or actively. It was a toxic situation and my mother was now 87 years old. He decided his own home; the house bought for him by her was infested with snakes and other poisonous creatures so moved back into her house. Increasingly frail following a stroke at 84 years of age, Lucy no longer had the resilience and resistance to survive. He consumed her 'meals on wheels' home-delivered food, demanded she wash and clean for him.

He was a tyrant in the household. Carers who came to shower Lucy three times weekly grew increasingly concerned for her well-being in that environment. Living three hours south of Perth, I visited as often as I could, cleaned the house and took my mother to medical appointments. I wanted her to move in to a retirement village but she refused concerned again about Jack's well-being and 'what would happen to him if she left'. Neighbours became concerned for her well-being. I rang almost daily and one evening and morning there was no response, which was atypical of our mother who lived her life according to clockwork. Finally, Jack answered saying she had collapsed and was in bed.

This was the beginning of a profound turning point in her life. I immediately ordered an ambulance and drove to the hospital in Perth where she had been admitted for observation following a seizure. In that day, she had three very bad seizures and the medical staff informed me she was dying. I rang my brother and asked him to come in and he replied that he would only come and see her if he was paid $30,000 which was typical of his disordered conversation about my mother at that time. He told me he had been 'fixing her up' with prescribed medications because one of his delusions was that he was a medical practitioner. I thanked him for his offer but politely refused his help.

My children arrived, now 12 and16 years, her only grandchildren, whom she loved dearly and whom had been the bright lights in the preceding 20 years in her life. She had treasured them, loved them ceaselessly and babysat them with a patience, kindness, warmth, softness and joy that I had never seen in her as a child. In fact, at times, I was quite 'miffed' that she brought them treats and allowed them so many freedoms that I was never allowed in my childhood. They adored her and every visit to Perth was special because of the time spent with 'Nana'. They were devoted to both her and her sister Rosanna. They gave many hours to entertain them with games, puzzles, artistic activities, shopping, walking, and the like. When I had worked during my son's early months, my mother had spent days caring for him and bringing him for feeds in between my teaching classes. Nothing was spared in her heart to care for him. So great was the caring bond between them that my son at 15 years of age, not brought up with any church attending rituals, would always wake at 7.00 am on Sunday to walk with Nana to mass to make sure she was all right. My daughter wrote her endless love letters, made her presents and showed warmth towards her that I could never find to give. By the time they arrived at the hospital their beloved nana had died. I was sitting next to her praying all the prayers I ever knew that she be released from her suffering. I had held her hand during the final seizure when she was in such great pain and distress. I had sat with her during the last sacramental rites performed by the resident catholic priest. The doctors had declared her dead. We had been moved from the busy hospital ward to a single quiet room, the death vault I suppose one could call it with its eerie emptiness, grey walls and carpets, a very bloodless space. This was the death setting when my children arrived having just completed a two hour train journey and a taxi ride to the hospital. I never forget this moment as it is etched in my memory in golden letters, as these heightened moments of death and suffering tend to be written with indelible ink within one's blood, carried through the very breath itself. My son, John, with his voice turning into manhood, stood there and spoke to her lifeless form, "Nana, I love you," he said, "and thanks for all the treats you bought me that I wasn't supposed to have; for my new suit, my boots and all the good food you made me."

My daughter, who was very close to my mother spoke with the boundless love that has always been in her heart since the day she was born. "Nana, I love you so much, Nana I love you, I love you…" she kept repeating this while holding her grandmother's hand and suddenly from the lifeless form, there was movement and my mother stirred and opened one eye, then two eyes. Then said slowly but clearly, "Rachael, I have been a long, long way away…I am back now and I am so hungry…please get me something to eat." Perhaps it was her profound devotion to the Blessed Virgin Mary that had restored her life, perhaps a miracle, perhaps my daughter's great love for her but whatever the cause, however incomprehensible and inapprehensible, my mother was now living again. This was indisputable and I was standing in a place that defies facts, logic and rationality. I was standing in that unfathomable zone where anything is possible and everything is available.

I went out to the find the doctor to request a reassessment of my mother. He looked at me with disbelief as though I was hallucinating and was speechless when he arrived to see my mother alive, although not exactly in robust health. He was puzzled but when I asked him what had happened, he replied as though he had sought answers to that question many times himself. "We know a great deal about how the human body dies, but we know very little about how the human spirit dies. There are people who should be dead like your mother, but are alive, and people who should be alive but are dead." This was probably the profoundest testimony to Lucy's incredible spirit, her remarkable resilience and will to survive. She kept walking even through the most challenging conditions of her life. It was a bold statement that her life was not yet finished, that she had further business to complete. It was also testimony to the intense bond of love between her and my daughter. If I ever spoke sharply to my mother, even as a three year old child, Rachael would intervene and say, "Don't speak like that to Nana, be kind to her." The next morning, I arrived to see my mother smiling and eating a hearty breakfast, and when the priest arrived to do the morning rounds, he was quite puzzled by this 'apparition' of my mother eating breakfast. He quietly asked me, "Is not this the woman who died yesterday that I did the last sacramental rites for in this room?"

"Yes," I replied.

"Well, I suppose," he replied, "God has other plans for her."

God, the universe, her angel, her will or however one conceives it to be, certainly had other plans for Lucy. After the hospital staff were informed of my brother's attempts to medicate my mother which explained the extraordinary amounts of bizarre chemicals in her blood samples, I asked the hospital to ensure that his visits to her were supervised, so that no more un-prescribed drugs would be administered to her by him. This is a tall order in a busy urban hospital where staff are very busy and unable to monitor visitor movements. They agreed to do their best. My brother did make an attempted visit to the hospital, and he was caught with bags full of drugs trying to give them to my mother. The hospital staff now fearing for her survival and for her safety, made an immediate decision that she must be transferred to a distant safe location that my brother would not know about and would not have easy access to. A hospital committee including the doctor advised me that it would be unsafe to release her back to her home at all and at any time. She was now too frail to live alone and would need on-going care especially with the signs of early dementia that she had already begun to exhibit. Furthermore, the hospital could no longer guarantee her safety from attempts by my brother to drug her again. Immediate removal was required to the country.

Never in my life, would I have ever thought it likely that I would take my mother to live with me in her declining years, nor was it her expectation that I would. While I had deep appreciation as a parent myself for her endless work and commitment in my childhood to provide for us children, gratitude for her unfailing physical presence in my adult life whenever needed for babysitting or assistance in any physical way, I was not close to her. Yes, I had witnessed how blessed her presence had been in my children's lives, but I only spent time with her as duty required and to look after her immediate needs. Like her, I had always done the dutiful things, assisted her when required, taken her for medical appointments, helped her in her home, driven her when required to visit friends or relatives, as she never owned or drove a car, but there was never any warmth between us. Long ago in my early childhood when she used to call me 'the Devil's chief instigator' whenever my brother and I quarrelled, and labelled me as passionate and emotional just like my hopeless father,

I had decided that I was nothing like her. Our relationship was functional during my adult life and I appreciated her generous grand parenting of my children. However, many of our conversations centred on my brother Jack and his needs, and his latest behaviours or escapades. She barely knew where I worked, my achievements, my career or what I had done in my life, and never bothered to ask me. The neighbours did say that she was 'proud of me' but she never told me directly. I presumed she loved me by her physical deeds for me throughout my life, but I never experienced her presence as warm and loving. I had long ago decided that I was my father's daughter and had little in common with her. However, looking at her frail form and knowing that the choice I made was a life and death choice for her, I knew I had to protect her with every fibre of my being, every drop of my blood. I knew that unless she was in my care, she would die. I knew I was the only one who could provide 24 hours of vigilant care to protect her. Therefore, the decision was made that she would come to live with me in the country, ironically, near the same town in which she had spent her early childhood in Australia. She was immediately transferred to the local hospital there and shortly afterwards my home.

I arrived back to her home to clear, in five days, her 50 years of accumulated possessions. I found my brother lodged there with her bank books and will, certain that she had died and waiting to access her finances. He was stunned by the news of her ongoing recovery but still he refused to leave the house and return to his own house that she had purchased for his use. I did not argue, I proceeded to dispose of everything in the house, remove her essential possessions to my home, recycle the rest and when nothing was left, not even a teacup, or a spoon, a table or a chair my brother begrudgingly left, cursing me and threatening to 'get Lucy back into his matrix'. I immediately had the door locks changed and any of his remaining possessions delivered to his house. I advertised it as a rental. This house, the walls vibrant with 50 years of Lucy's history, much of it marred by violence, regret, pain and suffering was about to close its doors to her life. Yes, the walls also had stories of joy and happiness, of the beauty of nature and art. There were over 60 beautiful paintings of flowers and the spectacular Australian landscapes that my mother had painted over the 20 years of her retirement until her hands had become too shaky to hold a brush and pen, following her first stroke. There was her exquisite fine China, that she had bought when the budget allowed her, which I carefully packed and transported to my home, so she could still enjoy its beauty. The only furniture I kept was the treasured dressing table from my childhood dreams full of sparkling shining things which I knew my mother loved and which contained so many memories of her life in Perth. It was time for the house to move into new hands. I had not realised how much soul and heart she had given to the neighbourhood until I was out on the front verge, throwing away so much other surplus unrecyclable possessions into a big bin. Neighbour after neighbour came enquiring after her, with stories of the support and kindness she had given them or their children. The teacher, the confidant, the carer, the cake maker, the interpreter of government forms, the gardener of this neighbourhood was no longer. Their feelings of loss, etched on their faces were palpable. It was the end of an era both for the neighbourhood and for my mother Lucy.

Chapter 8
Peace at Last

Therefore, it came to pass that Lucy was completing her life cycle as she moved into her daughter's home near Donnybrook, the place of her childhood following her migration to Australia. Again, she was living in the Darling ranges, the rolling green hills to the east of the Western Australian coast. Here in the hills were the good memories of childhood, rolling down slopes and into creeks, collecting bunches of spider orchids and kangaroo paws, climbing trees and painting wattles and blue leschenaultia. All of these memories glistened in her eyes as she sat in the daughter's home. Lucy, felt young within herself although her now frail diminutive figure sitting in the chair belied her inner portrait of herself. Lucy, stoically faced the loss of the home she had lived in for 50 years, and her beloved possessions, but managed the change, like many others in her life, by insisting that the routines of her life continue like clockwork. Breakfast at 8 o'clock every morning, followed by morning tea at 10am, lunch at 12 noon, afternoon tea at 2.30pm and dinner at 5.00 pm. Deviations were not allowed, and she chided even her favourite carer, Bob, one morning when he arrived at 8.01am with, "Bob, you are one minute late." Routine gave her predictability, a sense of control over her life, a bulwark against her fears in an otherwise unpredictable world. Her close neighbour and newfound friend, Janet, understood her needs and would daily visit her at 5.00 pm just before the carer left which gave her a sense of security. Never before fearful of being alone, Lucy now became very agitated if alone.

My mother lived with myself and my two adolescent children, John and Rachael, for five years. She arrived vulnerable and weakened with the life she had known in the city. Her clothes reflected the sense of despair, some might call it depression, that had developed in the last few years in Perth, where her life was dominated by her son Jack's demands and her declining ability to stand up for her own needs. Her clothes were mostly black and grey and the majority of her conversation was negative. My daughter Rachael began a 'Get Nana positive' program, and Nana was given a beautiful tin and each day she had to write three things upon three separate pieces of paper that she was grateful for: ' I have eyes, I can see', 'I have a home to live in', 'I am loved by my grandchildren'. Rachael explained to her nana how negative talk and thoughts make you feel unwell so now was the time to think positively and feel happy again. Lucy meticulously continued this practice for 12 months with her jar full of the positives in her life, which she would read daily. Her attitude changed radically and instead of focusing upon the losses of her life or the regrets, she began to live and enjoy the present moment. Her clothing now became full of colours, blues, green violets, whites, mauves, pinks, reds that represented her new more positive, hopeful and embracing attitude to her life.

Jack continued to write letters to her asking for money and filled envelopes with hundreds of pills with detailed instructions of how we were to administer these to Lucy, but they were binned. As her EPA, I had advised Jack that no bills would be paid for him from her finances. He would have free rent, maintenance and rates for the house in which he lived. In essence, a very clear line in the sand was drawn and Jack abided by these clear boundaries. He was welcome to visit my mother but, in five years, did so only on one occasion. Yearly, I drove her to Perth for his birthday lunch where the conversation was usually around money. Initially she worried about Jack and he pre-occupied much of her thinking. She worried how he was coping with his life and what was his mental state.

Then, unexpectedly, one Saturday afternoon, she had a very bad fall, tripping over a mat in the house and ended up with a twisted leg and hip broken in three places. An ambulance was called by the carer. I was notified and emergency surgery proposed. She was 87 years of age and the surgeon warned it was possible she would not survive as the breaks would require extensive repair. If successful, it would be at least three months before she could walk again. While re-locating her to a C class hospital was suggested, I had seen her sister at the same age in a 'C' class hospital suffer a broken hip and never walk again. She had died at 92 with horrendous bedsores. I made the decision that if she survived, we would nurse her at home, although I worked full time. The operation was successful but Lucy's mental state collapsed. She screamed if touched, threw herself off the bed if unsupervised and pulled out any tubes attached to her body. Intermittently, she would scream, "AAIIEE, AIIEE, AIIEE." I knew then, as I looked into her eyes that she was living her mother's tortuous death, triggered by her own close brush with death and the collapse of the defence mechanisms she had so long used to repress the memories. Fortunately, my mother's savings were able to pay for 24/7 carers around her bed in hospital to hold her hand and comfort her. Only then would she become tranquil. When she was finally discharged and home, again she would insist that she was dying, despite continuing to eat voraciously. The AAIIEE, AAIIEE, AAIIEE chanting now flared up again and she refused showers or to leave her bed. In the night hours, she would wake up screaming 'the title deed, the title deeds'. Lucy was caught in the morass of fear, terror, and uncertainty that had been repressed in her mind for over 80 years. There seemed no relief from these devilish torments. We were all in her hell realms. Two of us were needed five times a night to lift her out of bed to toilet, and Rachael and John, her grandchildren, devotedly woke many times a night to take their shifts, with love, tenderness and kindness. In between her fitful slumbers, she ruminated in torment. Somewhere, somehow, perhaps it was my grandmother's spirit in my blood, I made the decision that she would live, if I had to drag her back to life. Janet, her close friend and carer during much of her time in hospital, agreed that we would bring her back to a normal life. There were broken conversations with her about the 'title deeds' and her mother's murder, and for the first time in her life she began to speak about these moments. We would counter the AAIIEE, AAIIEE, AAIIEE moments by holding her hand and assuring her she was safe and protected. She was never alone. The fear of abandonment at her mother's death must have been so overriding that even the thought of being alone was sufficient to trigger her agitation.

Lucy had always loved food, so this was the primary motivator to get her out of bed and back to life. Despite her fall, her appetite and interest in food remained robust. Every day her food was placed further and further away from her bed, until it was actually on the dining room table. She moaned and complained about having to move towards it with her frame but the exercise five times a day changed her mental state. She decided she would live. Lucy agreed to showers and began doing her physiotherapy exercises with a rigor and attention to detail that even shocked the carers. Lucy's will to live and surmount obstacles had returned, and she was ready to continue to enjoy her life. Soon, she was walking 20 metres and one day when the carers failed to appear for breakfast, she walked 40 metres up a sharply inclined gravel road to her neighbours in search of Janet, whom she hoped would give her breakfast. A similar process was used to overcome the UTI's that she had lived with consistently on and off for ten years. She drank only one cup of black coffee a day, whereas five glasses of fluid was the recommended minimum. This meant that she had to drink one glass of fluid with each meal and to which she was highly resistant. Lucy's life and body always responded well to new routines, thanks to her lifelong adherence to them. Therefore, the solution was again simple. Her walking frame was removed from the table until the glass of liquid had been drunk. Following a week of loud protests, the new routine was established and the UTI's disappeared. It was strange but I began to notice how many similar characteristics I shared with my mother. There was this clinical commitment to proper routine, exercise and food.

When I found her eating lollies before breakfast, I would reprimand her with, "You know you don't eat sweets before meals," exactly what she would have said to me. But she was different now, and had abandoned these sorts of standards and would joke, "Ahh…but they taste better before meals than after meals." She developed a liking for chocolate and refused to eat her greens like her broccoli, something I could not ever imagine my mother doing as she was so strict with us about good food in our childhood. I would chide her, "You know my mother would never approve of eating chocolate instead of greens." Then she would ignore me as if she had not heard.

As weeks turned into months and years, I noticed I had her sense of duty, her love of beauty, her generous embrace of all family members, her determination and her ferocious will. I decided I must discover this Sicilian ancestry in my blood, which I had denied for so many years. I was 55 years of age, my mother was 89. I asked her to come back to Sicily with me for a visit. However, she responded that she was too frail to travel and besides she had revisited it nine years ago when she was 80. I regretted refusing the invitation to travel back with her then. I regretted all the times I had closed off conversations about Sicily, spurned it as a place to leave, not to a place to live and had ridiculed it to my mother whenever she tried to share her childhood experiences there with me. My dear neighbour Janet and my daughter Rachel would come too. We would go for four weeks and while there I would also provide lectures at the University of Enna. I shall never forget the moment the plane was close to landing in Catania with the majestic backdrop of Mt Etna and the azure blue Ionian Sea. I wept uncontrollably as if all my Sicilian ancestors were welcoming me home. I quickly noticed half the women in Sicily had hair like me, hair that I had been so ridiculed for as a child because of its extreme curl, somewhere between European and North African hair, which of course was Sicilian. I spoke no Italian, as a refugee from the Enemy Alien Act which denied Italian language to my mother. Often, I had asked her to teach me as a child but she refused to speak it to me, as she believed 'it was not safe to speak Italian' in

Australia. In Sicily, I knew I was at home and, in my motherland. The people I knew in my soul, the rhythms of the language in my ears, the culture was in my heart and the food tasted exactly right. It was strange how despite the mountainous nature of the country, it was embraced by the many eucalypts growing through the island. I visited my mother's childhood, home, remnants of the shop, the vineyards and chestnut forests, now covered by buildings. I searched the 'Chimetara' for my grandmother's grave and stood at the foot of the church where my mother had stood so many years before me. Everywhere that I trod in my mother's country, I sensed pieces of her heart in the land and I sent them back to her. It was as though they had been waiting for me to come and find them. I found them in Monterosso, in Pisano where she lived with her aunt and uncle, and in Messina. I met my mother's relatives, mostly my second cousins and despite language barriers, it was a celebration of joy and homecoming. We shared magnificent meals, and wonderful visits to places like Taormina and Etna Zafferano. My cousins teased me for looking so like my grandmother's sister Lucia, after whom my mother had been named. I saw a photo of her and I was awe struck by the resemblance.

I returned to Australia, on fire, determined to return to Sicily and live there with my mother. I enthusiastically spoke of the wonders of my Sicilian visit to my mother and proposed the migration plan of 'moving back to Sicily'. My mother looked at me puzzled and without hesitation replied, "I am Australian, and this is my home. I want to die here. I belong to this country." I was speechless. At last, I had discovered my motherland, I wanted to live there and become familiar with her, but my mother had left permanently. I argued with her. She said it was a poor country, I argued that it had Euros which were more valuable than Australian dollars. She said it was too close to invaders and wars but I assured her it was safe today. She looked at me with that look of bewilderment and astonishment that she reserved for my behaviours which she often found mysterious. Like my veganism. Here I was eating beans, nuts and vegetables, the poor person's diet in

Sicily. Here I was living voluntarily in the countryside, not because I had to farm the land but because I liked the country. She had studied so hard to achieve a professional occupation and live in the city. My behaviours frequently defied her rational world and its values. I knew the irrationality of my urge to migrate, but I also sensed the pulsing of the Sicilian country in my veins and in my blood. I tried to obtain an Italian passport but it was refused because my mother had abrogated her Italian citizenship in 1944 when she became naturalised.

Lucy's life work and energy had been deeply invested in Australia. She was proud of her teaching accomplishments and this was frequently reinforced by the school reunions she was invited to around the countryside. Whenever I accompanied her, I was amazed and delighted by the adulation of these now senior men and women for her work as a teacher in their communities, when they were children. Lucy saw her value in her teaching work and wrote a book chronicling the many schools at which she served as a teacher. She carried it with her everywhere and multiple copies. Once during a hearing test, the audiologist proceeded to tell her how little hearing she had in her left ear and how damaged her hearing in her right ear had become and he offered her a choice of hearing aids. Lucy's response was typical of her feisty spirit, "Listen, young man, you need to read this book (thrusting her teaching career book into his hands) I have done many things using my ears, and I don't need hearing aids now. If you insist on fitting them, I will flush them down the toilet when I return home or throw them out of my bedroom window." So often, her sense of value in life came from the decades of teaching in which she had inspired many young hearts and minds with her love of the beautiful, the good, worthy knowledge and the mastery of literacy and numeracy skills.

Her life in North Perth was becoming ancient history as she reunited with her Italian community in the south west, now peopled by seniors whom she had once played with as a child. Once a week, she now attended Italian club for the day, which she loved because her favourite niece also attended and devotedly assisted her so that she would become familiar with the routines. There she re-lived for a few years the embracing warmth and laughter of the Italian seniors. She was 88 years of age when, for the first time in her life, she fell in love with a man, other than my father, a man called Giuseppe who also attended the Italian club. He was 99 years of age and from a Sicilian village not far from where she had grown up. We heard Giuseppe's praise on a regular basis: His skin was so smooth, he walked without a frame, he always dressed smartly and looked debonair in his suit, and his manners were impeccable. Of course, she never shared her love with Giuseppe; it simply remained in her heart reminding her of her womanhood. However, they shared the same carer who transported them both to and from the Italian club, and when she returned home her footsteps seemed lighter, her smile brighter and her chatter more joyful. All around her now she re-experienced and reviewed her early life as we visited her old home, the cemetery where her father and two older sisters had been laid to rest, and her life teaching in so many of the one teacher schools.

Some quiet days when I would take her to Donnybrook for afternoon tea, we would pass the now extremely wealthy orchardist who once offered his hand to her in marriage. She would never have needed to work in her life and he would have assured her of a very wealthy comfortable family life within her own culture. When I would ask her how she now experienced rejecting his offer. She would reply without hesitation, "I was meant to meet your father and marry him, and have you children. I was meant to be a teacher and work for many years educating young children. I have done what I came to do and I have done it to the best of my ability." This was so typical of her stoicism, her belief that life throws you boomerangs from time to time and you need to do your best to learn how to master the skill to rise to the new challenges and succeed. That was the way it was with my mother, a stoical acceptance that life is as it is, that complaints and regrets are pointless, futile and worthless in the universe in which we live. There are deities like the Blessed Virgin Mary who care for us and help us through the challenges of our existence but they do not circumvent our life destiny, rather they stand as divine help and resources along the journey that has been laid out for our life. Lucy was devoted to Mary, but in the classical, spiritual and humanistic sense, religion was manifest in our day-to-day relationships with our neighbours, our workers, our students and our family. The place of action is in the human world, not in some far distant spiritual cosmos. The realm where we manifest is in our human life, for it is here that the signature of spirituality is written, in the way we treat our fellow workers, our students, our family, our friends and the public. It is here, in the human world, in our relationships that we live out of our ethics, our honesty, integrity, kindness and generosity. It is here that we see not human differences but human commonalities, and we embrace human diversity because despite differences we share a common humanity. It was her father's creed and it formed the significant pillar in Lucy's life.

At last, the dementia caught up with my mother. She was 90 years of age and she drifted in and out of her memories, her sensory experiences and the realities around her. Some days I was her mother, other days her sister Rosanna, and sometimes I was Trish. Jack, her son, had disappeared from her memory. Len came and went in a tranquil way. John had gone to university and achieved a Rhodes Scholarship and although she knew this was important, it had now slipped her memory that once this had been the crown of her aspirations for me. She no longer understood its meaning or implications. It was like that daily…little insight into her decisions but a real knowing at the bodily cell level, that she was surrounded by people who loved her and with whom she was safe and protected. In particular, she loved Rachael dearly and even when she could no longer remember her name, she always referred to her as 'the lovely kind girl, the one I want to talk to'. They spent many hours chatting between 11.00 pm and 2.00 am when Lucy woke up from her first round of sleep and, Rachael, the permanent night owl was still awake. It was

Rachael alone that finally convinced Lucy, not through argument but through warmth, that she was lovable simply for herself, not for her accomplishments or her deeds. Against all her defences that Lucy had created to survive the family wars of childhood, the only person who was able to dismantle those, even in this prolonged period of peace, was Rachael. Rachael showed her a warmth and love that she delighted in. I knew she also wanted it from me, but we were never able to break the pattern of my childhood, where I remained behind a barricade protecting my childhood heart from her efficiency and duty. I was too like her in that way, and the warmth between us had died so long ago. One moment there was a glimpse of it, before the dementia set in. She gently reached out and held my hand one evening, while I was helping her to bed, and quietly said, "Thank you for caring for me and taking me into your home." She smiled a special smile and there was a communion of love and warmth between us, before we retreated to the familiar ground where we expressed our love through duty, kindness, care, and generosity. In such deeds, our love was inscribed. We were able to express it in this way through the defences against our sensitivities.

The fifteen minute rhythm of the church bells in the little village of Monterosso, at the foot of Mount Etna remained in my mother's body till the day she died. Despite her dementia, she never failed to be meticulously on time for her meals, and always rose and went to sleep according to the exact hour of her sleeping rhythm. She did not remember if she had eaten a meal, but her body remembered the sounding of the rhythms of daily time and it moved in unison with them like an ancient dance in her blood. Her ancestors had breathed in these rhythms, they were in her breathing, not in her mind. Only death would cause them to cease. Following a severe stroke at 91 years, she survived just four weeks before passing away from pneumonia. Her spirit knew that she had completed her destiny, and I saw it in her eyes before she passed. I showed her the funeral service paper from her sister Rosanna's funeral service. There was a flicker of recognition in her eyes, a sorrow in her voice and her body shook as she quietly replied,

"So sad. I did love her." At that moment, I saw in her eyes that her life's purpose was finished. The next day, she was ill and transferred to palliative care where she died a week later in Bunbury, the town in which she had begun her teaching career. Her dying was tranquil. Many, many Sicilians who knew her came to visit, the room and her bed were sprinkled in rose petals and the air beautifully scented by them. Without pain and in the presence of those who most loved her, she gradually gathered herself for her next journey, beyond the broken down body she was now inhabiting. Her dearest friend and neighbour Janet came to sit by her bedside and be with her to her last breath.

It was natural that she was buried in the Catholic cemetery in Donnybrook, little Sicily as it is known, where her father, older sisters and other relatives' remains have been laid to rest. They gave their life, their labour and their blood for this new country. They made it their home. Following an inspiring requiem mass and a splendid feast of a wake which Lucy would have wholeheartedly approved, she was buried in this little forest cemetery surrounded by eucalypt trees, kangaroo paws and wattle, in the soil of the country she too had made her home.

Rest in Peace.